THE MAP THAT CAN TWIST TIME

THE MAGIC PEOPLE - BOOK 2

ANDI CUMBO-FLOYD

For the people of the Blue Ridge Mountains who were displaced by the creation of the Shenandoah National Park and Skyline Drive AND for the those of us who love the park and the Drive.

May we all remember.

1

The air was as hot and thick as cat's fur, but in the lake, Jed and Charlie didn't much care. I, however, was fanning myself with a copy of *Better Homes and Gardens* from 2006 that I had found on the coffee table in the cabin the Wilsons had rented for the week. I am not a fan of summer. Nope, not a bit. Give me a January day anytime. I can always put on more clothes, but for the sake of decency, there's only so much a person can take off.

Still, the evening was pleasant, with the heat and humidity giving way to the lake breeze. The day was turning over to the purple of night, and as the boys climbed out of the lake, I watched the fireflies begin to flicker in the tree line. Behind me, I could hear the faint voices of Mr. and Mrs. Wilson as they had their one beer each and grilled hamburgers up on the deck at the cabin. *This is about perfect*, I thought.

I immediately regretted letting my thoughts go that far to good. All my 63, almost 64, years had taught me that the world worked —Lord or no—in mysterious ways. You never knew what might jinx a perfectly good night such as this.

I was happy though; I was. It had been a few months since Jed and I'd had our adventure with the HeavenLand folks and since Charlie had come to live with the Wilsons after his own daddy had cut him off. These days had been good ones, even if it had taken a bit of getting used to having everybody seeing me and all. I'd been imaginary for many years, and if I were honest, I sometimes missed the days when it was just Jed and me. Or maybe, I just kind of missed having Jed all to myself in a way.

But I did like how when I talked with folks, they looked me in the eye, and I really liked to choose my seat at the movies and not have to move if someone accidentally sat down on me. It could be pretty awkward to have someone plop down in your lap, a little too personal, if you know what I mean.

I wasn't thinking about all that by the lake that night though. Nope, I was just relaxing in one of those Adirondack chairs that look like they'd be super comfortable but are really just torture to get out of. The boys ran around and scooped fireflies out of the air. It was quiet, comfortable, easy . . . And so, the sound of the bells came through the air crisp and clear.

If it had been winter, I would have thought the bells signified the arrival of Santa . . . or maybe that White Witch woman from Narnia—that was Jed's favorite book series when he was a kid, but that woman scared the bejeezus out of me. But in summer, my first thought was *ice cream truck*, and that almost made the awkward climb out of my chair worth it.

Jed, Charlie, and I turned our faces toward the road, and Jed asked, "What is that?"

Charlie said, "Wagon."

I looked at Jed, and then he looked at Charlie. "Wagon?"

"Yeah, those are horse bells. Lots of wagons use them. Help keep the wagon trains together at night, especially if it gets foggy."

Charlie would know, seeing as how he'd grown up in the age of wagons and all.

Then, as if on cue, the fog rolled in across the lake, and I knew it. I'd jinxed the night. Me and my ridiculous optimism.

Around the bend in the road and from behind the house next door, a wagon rode up out of the fog. But not just any wagon. This one looked like the old-timey version of a camper, all wood and painted on the sides. A man sat hunched over the reins on the front bench, and even from where I stood, I could tell he was exhausted. I worried he might fall asleep right then and there.

But instead, he pulled up a little on the reins, and his two small horses stopped. He gave them each a good scratch on the rump and then climbed down to the ground. Only then did he look up and say, "I've been looking for you three all over time. When I finally stopped to ask directions, Shelby said I'd find you here."

Jed gave me a quick look and then jogged over to help the man lift a huge trunk out of the back of the wagon. That boy would carry the Mona Lisa if a thief needed help stealing it. Sometimes, his helpfulness really irked me. We did *not* need whatever was in that trunk; I could tell you that.

"Shelby sent you to us?" Charlie had taken the other end of the trunk, and they were headed toward the cabin after the man had pointed that direction.

"Wait, boys." I'd finally begun to understand that my age gave me a sort of authority with most folks and that it also made people think I was responsible for these kids. The man looked up at me expectantly, but the boys kept on toward the cabin. Okay, other people thought I had authority; Jed and Charlie had no such delusions. "Jed, Charlie. Set that trunk down." This time, the shrill edge to my voice got to them, I guess, because they dropped the trunk with a thud.

"Sir, forgive me for asking, but I expect you can understand we might be a bit leery of somebody just rolling up and asking us to carry a heavy object into our house."

The man looked at me out of the corner of his eye, and then I saw him wink at Jed. "You think I'm delivering a bomb, missy?" He turned to me with a grin then.

I sputtered a bit. "Well, no, sir. I am a bit surprised you know what a bomb is though." His wagon had made me imagine he was from a time before cars, and I was pretty sure that bombs didn't predate cars. Maybe? I never was very good with history.

"Don't let my wheels fool you, Mavis. You know better than to think that just because a person looks one kind of way that they are that way."

I felt myself blush. He was right about that. Our travels through time and around the world had taught me that through and through, and yet, here I was, forgetting everything I'd learned.

I blamed the fireflies. They had distracted me.

Charlie, never one to bother too much with manners, did me the favor of asking what I wanted to know though. "What's in the trunk, mister?"

"Name's Hercules, son. And we'll need to open that inside to answer that question."

I looked carefully at Hercules. He was small, wiry almost, and since he had gotten off of that wagon, he didn't look quite so tired. His head was slick in the middle, and his shiny brown skin was surrounded by a thin ring of steel-gray hair. If I hadn't known better, I'd think he was quite old, but as Hercules himself had just reminded me, I did know better.

I gave Jed a little nod, and he and Charlie carried the trunk up onto the deck, where Mr. and Mrs. Wilson waited. I hung back to get a closer look at that wagon, but I still heard the Wilsons intro-duce themselves and invite Hercules for burgers. You couldn't blame Jed for being helpful. His parents would invite the art thief over to dinner after Jed helped him carry out his spoils.

I made my way over to the horses, giving them a little scratch behind the ears as I circled around to read the wagon's side. "Hercules Pettit—Peddler of All the Things You Never Knew You Needed."

Peddler. I'd heard of them, but I'd imagined they drove wagons that rattled along with pots and pans and a random accordion hanging off the side, not this tidy, pretty thing. I was intrigued though . . . *all the things I never knew I needed*. I imagined there was a whole world full of them, and I wasn't sure I liked the idea that someone could bring them to me. Wasn't sure I liked that at all.

2

The Wilsons had decided a couple of weeks back that we all needed a little break from the farm. The Heaven-Land folks came and went as they pleased, and they helped keep the crops going and the chickens fed. But they had their own business to attend to, and while I had really hoped Cato and Squeak might come along with us, Shelby had said they needed to stay back—let our family have a little alone time. She was being really nice by including Charlie and me as part of the Wilson family since Charlie and I weren't really a part of it. At least Charlie was officially their foster child. I was just the old lady who had appeared out of nowhere one day.

When the Wilsons said we were headed into the mountains for a couple of weeks, I'd offered to stay back and mind the farm, but Mrs. Wilson had given me a look that threatened to peel back my eyelids until I agreed, so I'd come along. "You'll always be family, Mavis," she'd told me as I'd put my bag in the turtle-shell carrier on the car roof. I wanted to believe her; I really did.

Now, though, I kind of wished I'd pushed harder to stay home. I could not see how an old-fashioned peddler who specialized in the unexpected could be a good thing. We'd already had a lot of "unexpected" this year. I figured we—especially the Wilsons—were due for some straight-up "expected."

I had planned to pull Mrs. Wilson aside when I got into the cabin, warn her about what the wagon said, but the places were already set, and Hercules was seated at the other end of the farm table across from Mr. Wilson. I was too late.

"What brings you here, um, Mr. . . ." Mr. Wilson stumbled over his words as he slid hamburger patties onto the tray of toasted buns.

"Hercules is just fine, sir. The kids can call me Uncle Hercules if they'd like. Folks around here don't take too well to kids calling old folks by just their first names. Don't bother me no mind though."

Mrs. Wilson gave the old man a warm smile. "Hercules is just fine with us. We want our children to learn to call people by the names people use for themselves. That's true respect as we see it." She winked at me then, and I grinned back. I always loved that she'd never minded her son's imaginary friend for all these years was old enough to be his grandmother.

As the plates of burgers, coleslaw, baked beans, and carrot sticks made their way around the table, Charlie spoke up. "Hercules had us carry in a big heavy trunk. Said he was dropping it off for us, the Wilson family. Ain't that right?" Charlie looked at the peddler with a grin.

"That's right, son. That trunk is just what you folks are going to be needing long about"—he took a gold pocket watch from his vest pocket—"oh, seven thirty in the morning, give or take."

Jed pushed his chair back from the table, and I could tell he was headed for that trunk. But Mrs. Wilson gave that you-know-better look again, and Jed sat back down, shoulders hunched but mouth shut. He knew better.

"So what is it you do, Hercules?" Mr. Wilson said before he took a bite of a burger so big it looked like he might have to unhinge his jaw.

"Oh, well, I guess I'm a delivery man of sorts. I bring people the things they need."

"So that's your power then?" Jed's mouth was full of slaw, and I thought his mother might smack his hand for poor manners.

Hercules gave Jed a thin smile. "I don't know that I'd call it a 'power' really. Reckon some folks call it a gift. Me, it's just what it has always been. 'Spect you know a bit about that yourself."

Jed gave the old man a knowing nod, a nod that seemed much older than his twelve years, and then he tucked into his burger like he might die if it didn't reach his stomach in the next 1.2 seconds.

"Mavis, something special in there for you." I jerked my gaze over to Hercules then. "Be sure to check in the left-hand side pocket. That's the left-hand side when you is looking at the trunk."

I swallowed my mouthful of baked beans, knowing better than to incur the wrath of Mrs. Wilson, and said, "Something for me? But there must be some mistake. I'm not part of the Wilson family."

All three of the blood-related Wilsons started to speak at once, but Hercules cut them off. "Now Mavis, I've been a lot of places in a lot of times, and I can tell you this with the assurance of what some would say is too many years—family is made by claiming, not by no blood and not by some document some judge signs. Family is made by claiming," he said again as if I might have missed it, "them claiming you and you claiming them. So you stop that nonsense about not being a Wilson. Seems to me you all claimed one another pretty good."

I looked around the table then. I had to take a big swig of sweet tea to keep from crying.

The rest of dinner we talked about the places Hercules had been: Monaco, São Paolo, Athens—where he went by the name Heracles "just to get people good and confused"—and then Rome. "Got to thank Rick Riordan for helping folks get their gods and goddesses right. It's been a pain in the rear for a long time, but finally, things seem to be getting cleared up."

I wondered if he was hinting that he was a god. I couldn't get myself to ask the question, though, because it felt rude to have to ask a god if he was, well, a god and because if it was supposed to be obvious, I didn't want to look stupid. For whatever reason, I wanted to be my best self with this kind, smart old man. Ten minutes ago, I'd been ready to put him back on his wagon and send him off, but I'd learned that even a little bit of time with a person can change a mind right quick.

Too soon, though, Hercules pushed his chair back from the table and stood up. "Thank you so much for dinner, Mrs. and Mr. Wilson. It was just what I needed."

I glanced at his plate, and it was clean as a whistle although I couldn't remember him eating a single thing.

He slipped a derby hat on his head and headed toward the door. "That trunk now, it'll be about time for ya'll to open it right soon. You'll need some time to prepare, and of course, you'll also want a good night's sleep. Mavis, remember that left-hand pocket."

He gave a tiny bow as he walked out the door, and before I could take my next breath, I heard the bells ringing.

AFTER WE FINISHED CLEANING up the dinner dishes, we gathered around the trunk, and I finally got a good look at it. It looked like one of those old steamer trunks people were always bringing to

Antiques Roadshow because they thought they were worth something. *Spoiler alert—they aren't.* This trunk was brown with lots of straps crisscrossing it on all sides. On one side, there was a red sticker that looked a lot like an old-fashioned stamp, and it said "Paris" in faded letters.

The clasp was a simple metal one that had a keyhole and a little lever to push down to release it. For a second, I worried that we'd need the key, but when Jed reached over and pushed down the lever, the top popped open like it was on springs.

Inside, all I could see were clothes, warm clothes, clothes that looked like they were made of dead animals . . . I shivered. I wasn't the biggest fan of fur, but I figured this probably meant we were going somewhere cold. I smiled. Cold, cold I could handle.

By the time we finished unloading the trunk, we had five fur coats, five pairs of fur-lined boots, some mittens that looked like they were made from some sort of skin, and one of those caps with the ear flaps. I thought about claiming that for myself, but one look at Charlie's scrawny frame, and I knew that the boy needed all the help with body heat that he could get.

For a few minutes, it felt like an awkward adult dress-up party—just like the ones Jed and I used to have with the party dresses his mom's friends had given him and the plastic Spiderman costume leftover from Halloween. I'd always felt a little silly with one of those pink sparkly things tugged up one leg and over my forearm. The abundance of my hips limited my ability to actually put on most of the dresses. Plus, I wasn't really the cocktail dress type, my recent experience with a corset withstanding. I felt the same way now, a long fur coat draped over my shoulders, and the cuffs of the fur boots feeling creepily comfortable against my bare legs. Everyone was trying on everything, and I was doing my best to look like I was into the spirit of a new adventure.

But all I could think about was what Hercules had left me in that left-hand pouch. I could see the pocket, not very puffed out or anything, so I figured it wasn't more clothing. It was probably some sort of old lady thing—a pair of those spectacles with the earpieces that fold around your ears, or something. But the way the old man had talked, I didn't think I was going to like whatever it was—I had lived enough surprises already, and I wasn't really very keen on more.

I had learned, though, that there was no avoiding the path that life sets you on, so while Mrs. Wilson snapped a selfie of her and Jed in their fur coats, I slipped my hand into the pocket of the trunk and pulled out a thick fold of paper. I slid it into the back pocket of my jeans and donned my fur-lined mittens. I'd look at it later. Alone.

IT DIDN'T TAKE LONG for the enthusiasm over the fur attire to die down. The August heat, and the overall fatigue from hours in the sun and water had the boys dozing on the couch before eight o'clock. Mr. and Mrs. Wilson were cuddled up on the loveseat to watch their favorite movie, *You've Got Mail*. I was stretched out in the papasan chair that I was thinking of stealing and taking back to my yurt at the farm. I was trying to look relaxed, but I could practically feel that piece of paper burning against my rear end.

I feigned a yawn and said, "I'm going to head up to bed. This day has me knackered." I didn't know if it was my use of the word *knackered* for the first time ever or just an observational skill that came with motherhood, but Mrs. Wilson said, "You'll tell us about that paper in the morning?" She gave a little glance at my tuchus and winked.

I felt the color rise in my cheeks, and I gave her a nod. Nothing got by her.

I washed my face and brushed my teeth, put on my super comfy "I'll be your Huckleberry" grizzly bear pj's, and climbed into the not-so-comfy bed. I swore that bowling balls had lain completely still in that bed for decades before a human body had touched it.

I picked up the folded paper from the nightstand where I'd placed it before I took off my jeans, and I began to unfold it. Its thickness made me think it was folded in quarters, maybe eighths, but as I kept unfolding, the paper grew and grew in size until it was the width of my double bed and as long as my legs.

At first, it looked like it was blank, just a yellowed-out piece of paper that someone had tucked away to use later. But as I studied it, slowly, the shapes of the continents of the world began to come into view. The process reminded me of that invisible ink trick with lemon juice and a candle.

There was Africa, then Antarctica, then Australia, Asia, Europe, South America, and finally North America. I loved old maps, especially of places I knew, and so my eye drifted naturally to Virginia. It looked like itself, if a little wonky on the western edge, but there, just over the Blue Ridge, I could see a lighter spot. In fact, it looked like a glow.

I held the map up to the light, and the glow disappeared. Put it down in front of me, and it was back. I pulled the map closer to my face and watched as roadways and the names of towns began to appear. Then, as I squinted and put my nose almost to the paper, I could see, just where the glow was, a small lake, and a tiny cabin, and . . . I dropped the map then picked it right back up again. Yep, sure enough, if I let my eyes go just a little out of focus, I could see myself, right now, looking at the map . . . on the map. I set the map down and climbed into bed.

I felt like I was in one of those M.C. Escher paintings where a figure walks down the steps only to be going up the steps on the other side. So weird.

The fact that I could see that much detail about myself made me curious though, so I pulled the map up to my chest and took a gander at the only other place I knew—the Wilsons's farm. Sure enough, there were LaKeemba and Shelby by the bonfire as usual. I could see Alonso walking out by the tents, doing his nightly check on everybody. Cato and Squeak were there in their cots, sound asleep and drooling. I wanted to stare at my friends a while, but it felt wrong, like I was spying or something. So I let my eyes wander over the map some more.

That's when I saw it, a flicker down in the very tip of South America, another glow. This one was blue, though, like the light was coming from under water. I looked closer, but it felt like I was looking through a fog. I leaned farther in, and just as my eyelashes were about to hit the paper, I felt it, that same sensation of gentle movement I'd felt it when the old oak had walked me through time.

Then, I looked up and realized I was standing at the foot of an ice-blue glacier; at least I thought it was a glacier. It looked like the ones I'd seen in pictures. It rose up from the water at my feet and towered above me in spiky twists that reminded me of the meringue on a pie.

The site was spectacular, and I could have stared at it for hours . . . if I hadn't started to shiver. Hard. I looked around to see if there were someplace I could go to get out of the wind, but I didn't see any signs of human life: no houses, no cars, no nothing but water and ice and a stretch of gray-brown ground going off behind me as far as I could see.

I blew on my hands, making sure to keep the map tightly gripped in my ever-more-frozen fingers, and I wondered if going invisible would help, but I couldn't see how since my power didn't make me unseen *and* warm. Just unseen. I thought about walking inland because surely someone would be somewhere soon, right? Surely, most places on the earth were inhabited by humans by now, right?

I groaned. When was now, though? I could be in the dinosaur age or about to be stampeded by a herd of wooly mammoth for all I knew. Or maybe I was in some sort of *Star Trek*-like hologram in the future. I decided my best bet was to figure out how I'd gotten here and then reverse whatever I had done and get home.

The map looked the same as it had back at the cabin although this time South America wasn't as full of lines and towns, and the big word *Patagonia* spread across the part of the continent where I stood. There, right where I was, I imagined, was that golden glow. The blue light was gone, but I hoped that my only chance of getting home hadn't gone with it.

I pulled the map very close to my face and gazed at the Blue Ridge, trying to focus my eyes on exactly where the Wilson cabin was. For a moment, I thought it wasn't going to work, but then, the tug, and I was back in my bed. Same as it had been when I'd left.

I scrambled up and grabbed the three spare blankets I'd seen in the top of the closet when we'd arrived. I stretched them across my legs and kept my arms out just long enough to carefully fold the map and tuck it under the pillow next to me before cocooning myself in warmth as I pondered what exactly I had been supposed to see in Patagonia.

THE NEXT MORNING, the Wilsons were all eating pancakes with Nutella and bananas when I finally lumbered out of bed. "Nine thirty! Why didn't anyone wake me?"

Jed grinned. "We figured you needed your sleep after all that traveling."

I squinted at my best friend. "How did you know?" I shouldn't have asked because all I got as a response from Jed was a snicker as he slid another bite of pancake in his mouth. Honestly, these magic people just knew stuff in ways I didn't get . . . yet.

I plopped down in my chair at the side of the table and poured a slightly more than necessary amount of maple syrup on my pancakes. I never had gotten on board with hazelnut and chocolate on my pancakes . . . except for chocolate chips inside them, of course.

"So, Mavis, where are we headed?" Mr. Wilson was looking at me with a smile so big I thought his jaw might unhinge.

I looked at Jed, and he nodded. "We figured since there were five of everything in the trunk that we're all going. Dad's a little excited."

I glanced back at Mr. Wilson, and he looked like he'd just eaten way too much candy . . . or needed to pee. I wasn't sure if he was going to be as excited when I told him we were going to a frozen, isolated spot I'd never heard of, but I figured I might as well get it over with. "Patagonia." I looked down at my plate and carefully crafted the perfect bite of syrup and pancake while I waited for the groans to ensue.

"Are. You. Serious!" Jed's voice had gone about ten octaves higher. "Seriously, Mavis. You're not teasing, right?"

I had my mouth full of pancake, but it seemed important to immediately assure him I was serious. So I nodded vigorously and watched as Jed literally jumped up in the chair, climbed onto it, and did a little booty-shake. I almost blew the pancake across the table I was laughing so hard.

"You know there are rumors about giants there, right? Remember that show *Digging for the Truth*? They did a whole episode about them . . . and maybe we can see one . . ." He was literally jumping up and down. "I'm going to watch that episode right now so I'm all refreshed."

Charlie looked a bit stunned, but I couldn't tell if it was because Jed was bouncing like a monkey, because he had never heard of Patagonia, or because he still wasn't quite used to the idea of television yet.

"Jed," his mother called. "How are you going to watch it? Your DVDs are at home."

"I have it downloaded on my iPad." Jed's voice came from his bedroom.

Mrs. Wilson looked at me. "Well, alright then." She let out a soft sigh. "So Patagonia . . . that's exciting." She looked down at her plate and moved her fork around in the puddle of syrup left there. "Do you know *when* we are going?"

It was a good question and one I wished I could answer. From the lack of signs of human habitation I'd seen in my short visit last night, I could guess we were going back in time some ways, but how far back, I couldn't even begin to guess. Plus, it was possible that this was one of those rare spots on earth where people were very sparse. "I have no idea." I took one last bite of syrup-sopping pancake. "Let me get the map."

By the time I got back to the table, the dishwasher had been loaded, the extra pancakes wrapped in plastic wrap, and the table cleared. Jed's parents were a cleaning-up power couple.

I slowly unfolded the map and stretched it out across the table. Charlie grabbed stone coasters and set them at each corner, and then all four of us bent over the yellowed paper. It was blank again, and I feared this was going to be one of those things like in the movies where "invisible woman is the only one who can see the invisible map." But then, slowly, the outlines of the continents began to appear.

"Jed, you'll want to see this." Mr. Wilson bellowed down the hallway. "It's a map."

He must have said the magic words, because within a second, Jed was at the table and putting his nose right down near the paper.

I grabbed him by the shoulder and jerked him back. "Don't do that!"

"Ow. Do what? I was just looking."

"Oh, sorry. Yeah, just don't get your face too close. That's what caused me to travel last night." I looked down at the map. "I'm still not sure how this thing works."

Charlie was studying the American East Coast carefully, and before I knew it, he'd put his eye right down to the page. I braced myself, but nothing happened. "I can see the home place," Charlie said quietly before he stood up and walked silently out of the room.

I bent close over the part of Virginia where the plantation Charlie had been born stood, and there, I could just see the word "Poke"—Charlie's last name—written in a fine script. I couldn't even imagine what that might feel like for Charlie, who knew he could never go home.

But as I looked closer, I saw the Wilson farmhouse appear, too, almost superimposed over the *e* in "Poke." Then, as I watched, the words "Farm Haven" appeared next to a cluster of buildings somehow on top of but not obscuring the Wilson homestead.

"Hmm." Mrs. Wilson spoke from just behind my shoulder, "I've never heard of Farm Haven before. Have you, Leon?"

Mr. Wilson shook his head.

My eyes drifted a bit west, and there it was again—a golden, glowing dot. But this time, there were four other dots too; all glowing orbs of light huddled together right where we were in the Blue Ridge. "See there?" I pointed at the glow. "Each of those is one of us."

I could feel everyone's eyes trail mine, and then, Charlie, who had slipped back in, his eyes just slightly more red, said, "What's that blue dot?" He put his finger right on the spot in Patagonia, and like that, he was gone.

A gasp passed through the room, but we knew what we had to do. We donned our coats, mittens, boots, and Jed got to wear the ear-flap hat. Mr. Wilson tossed Charlie's coat and things over his arm, and together, we touched the blue dot while I held the map with one hand.

Just like that, we were back on the scarp of land I'd seen last night, the glacier bright and blue in front of us. Charlie was there, shivering away, but Mr. Wilson got him sorted straight off, and then, we huddled up in order to figure out what was next . . . and to conserve body heat. The furs were warm, but sometimes the knowledge of cold is just as powerful as the actual cold.

Jed, ever the king of the puzzle hunt, began theorizing right away. "Okay, so we know where are—at least roughly—but the question is about when we are. These coats and mittens were stitched with machines, at least I think so since the stitches are more even than they'd be if someone had hand-sewn them. Right, Mom?"

"Right, Jed."

"So if we imagine Hercules to be reliable in delivering what is necessary, we have to think we're in modern times, at least relatively, or everything we are wearing would be handmade," Jed continued. "So, maybe, this time we're not traveling in time, just in space."

I wasn't sure that theory actually held weight—after all, we had traveled in time, so couldn't things travel, too? I was about to point that out when the most beautiful and scary thing I'd ever seen came into view over Jed's left shoulder. A mammoth. A fluffy, furry, *huge* wooly mammoth that made Snuffleupagus look downright silly.

I managed to tear my eyes away from the creature and look at Jed. "I see what you mean, but there may be another reason. It may be that we aren't going to see any people who would know the difference." I pointed at the creature that was slowly but surely headed our way. "I think we need to hide."

Everyone followed the trail of my finger, and I saw the color pass out of their faces. It was a frantic search for shelter. We all split up, hoping for a cave, or tree line, or something, but since the land was so flat, we could see that there wasn't anything like that. That turned out to be a good thing, though, because if there had been anything between each of us, we might have lost each other. Instead, we were able to huddle up again, this time a bit farther from the mammoth.

The creature didn't look aggressive—at least it hadn't charged us yet. But it was also very curious and kept getting a bit closer every few moments. I didn't care if that creature just wanted a snuggle. It was ginormous, and I was fairly sure it would crush me with one foot if it tried to give me a hug.

"Okay, don't panic." Mr. Wilson's voice was calm but clipped. "We're going to figure something out."

I so appreciated his vote of confidence, but I didn't see quite how that could be . . . until the map rustled in my pocket. I pulled it out and began to unfold it. We could just touch the map and go home.

Just then, a hand fell heavy on my shoulder, and I looked up to see Alonso, our friend from HeavenLand. His presence made me calm down, but I also wondered if he wasn't giving me a dose of his own soul-boosting magic. It didn't matter. I was just so glad to see him. "I wouldn't do that, Mavis. If you go back now, you'll miss it."

"Miss what?" I didn't want to sound annoyed, but even I could hear the shrillness in my voice. I figured nothing would be worth facing off against a mammoth. I figured wrong.

"Miss that." Alonso pointed out toward the glacier, and there, rising from the water like it were on a stage at a rock concert, was a ship. But not like any ship I'd ever seen. It was half submarine with its rounded front and long cylinder of a body and half tall ship with three masts standing proud from the flat deck. That wasn't the strangest part, though. What was really strange was that it was made of ice . . . or at least it looked like it was. The entire ship was the same shade of blue as the glacier, that kind of blue that looks so cold it would hurt to touch it.

Charlie let out a long whistle, and I grabbed hold of Alonso's wrist. Jed took several slow steps forward until his dad grabbed his shoulder and kept him from sliding into the water.

"See?" Alonso was looking at me with a sly grin that I half wanted to wipe off his face and half wanted to hug him for.

"What is it?" My voice was hushed, but it still carried across the still landscape. It was only then I realized the boat was not actually in the water. It was floating just above it. The world spun a bit until Alonso righted me with an arm around my shoulders.

"It's your ride, Mavis."

I looked at my friend and then back at the boat and then at Alonso again. "Our ride where?"

"Back home."

Now, I was thoroughly confused. I could get back home through the map, as Alonso clearly knew since he'd stopped me from using it a few moments before. So why did I need this ship?

A voice from the deck of the boat said, "You need us because we are the fastest transport in the now."

I looked up to see Lakeemba, Shelby, and Sharon on the prow; the brown skin of my friends from HeavenLand practically shimmered against all that ice blue. "We'll explain later, everyone." LaKeemba's voice was as officious as ever. "Now, though, we need to move on." She gave a quick glance behind her and then motioned for Marcus to lower a ladder for us as the boat pulled up next to the land as if the earth were a dock.

"It's floating," Mrs. Wilson whispered.

"That's what things do on water, Mom." Jed was already halfway up the ladder.

"No, I mean it's floating in the air."

I saw Jed's left foot stutter before it found footing again on the rung he'd just left. He looked down, and all the color washed right out of his face.

"Later, Jed." Sharon's tone was serious, and it got Jed moving.

Soon, we were all up the ladder, and the ship was moving swiftly—how, exactly, I had no idea, because I couldn't hear an engine or see any oars. But every time I opened my mouth to ask a question, Shelby, LaKeemba or Sharon gave me a look that silenced me immediately.

Later, I thought to myself. As we pulled away from shore, I watched the mammoth watching us. I could swear it looked a little sad.

After we were well underway and Sharon had brought us all mugs of hot cocoa, we all settled into a warm cozy cabin—still seemingly made of ice—below deck while Marcus took over the ship. "It's not just horses you have a way with, huh?" I had whispered as I gave him a quick hug.

"No, ma'am, it certainly is not," he had said with a grin as he turned back to the captain's wheel. The wheel looked like it could have been an ice sculpture at someone's pirate-themed wedding.

"Now that you are here, we have work to do." Shelby pulled out a notebook with a brightly-colored owl on the cover and flipped to a blank page. "Tell me everything you know about the place where your cabin is located."

Mr. and Mrs. Wilson exchanged looks, but then Mr. Wilson said, "Not much. We know that it was once a thriving town, back before the Shenandoah National Park came through and displaced the people who lived there. I've seen pictures of stores and schools, farms with huge gardens and pig pens. We stopped by the historical society outside the park before we went up."

I had loved every minute of the historical society with their little miniature homestead that had been the childhood home of one of Virginia's governors and the old dresses that gave me flash-backs to a few months earlier at Charlie's plantation. But we hadn't stayed long because it looked like Jed and Charlie might mutiny if we didn't get moving.

Mrs. Wilson nodded and then added, "But we don't know just where our cabin is in relation to those places. I'm not sure if it ever was part of the town Capers or not. Or if it's always been kind of remote, separate, you know."

Shelby nodded as she took down notes. "Do you know anything about who lived in the actual cabin?"

"Not a thing," Mrs. Wilson said.

Charlie spoke up. "Actually, I know a little bit."

We all looked at him. How could he know more than we did?

I saw pink tinge the top of his ears. "I found a diary."

LaKeemba gave him a small nod, and I saw him square his shoulders.

"I'm sorry. I probably should have told you, but I kind of just wanted something small of my own."

I couldn't blame the kid. He'd lost everything and everyone he'd known when he'd come with us. Still, I was surprised he'd been able to keep it secret. Charlie wasn't exactly one to parse his words.

Mrs. Wilson rubbed small circles on his back, and he settled back into the cushioned bench beside her. "I found it under this loose board in my room. I used to hide my marbles and things under a board at the old place, so when it creaked, I wondered if someone else had done that too."

"What does the journal say, Charlie?"

"It's a diary by a woman named Ruth. She talks about boys a lot, I mean men—she's old, like twenty. She keeps calling herself a spinster." The pink tint returned to his ears. "But the interesting part is when she talks about the walkers, how they come into the woods behind the cabin from everywhere. She recognized them right away because—here's the good part—she was a walker herself."

That little piece of information got everybody stirred up. Another magic person had lived in the cabin, and she'd known she could travel in time. All of us had theories to share, and we all started talking at once.

"That's not all, though," Charlie almost had to shout to get our attention. "She said she'd lived over the mountain for a while, sounded like she might have been over by where I grew up." He looked at Jed. "I mean, where you grew up too."

That was interesting, but not really crucial at the moment.

Shelby was scribbling as fast as she could, but she stopped long enough to ask, "Anything else?"

"Well, she mentioned Hercules."

Jed and I both leaned forward. "The peddler," I whispered.

Charlie gave a slow nod. "I wasn't sure at first, but given that this is a ship from the future, and he brought us a trunk to take us to it, I figure he must be a time walker too."

Everyone else nodded along like Charlie had simply told them dinner was ready, but I was not going to let that one slide by. "Did you say this ship is from the future?"

Sharon chuckled. "He's right, Mavis. It is."

My mouth fell open . . . That explained a lot—well, mostly everything—about it. Except for how Charlie knew that. "How did you know?" I gave Charlie a hard look.

"How did you not know, Mavis?"

This time, it was my ears that turned pink. I took a sip of my cocoa and waited.

"You are on a ship from 2663. You don't need to know much except that it runs on water and will disappear in seventy-two hours. These things are not made to be permanent. So we have limited time." LaKeemba's voice was kind but firm. "Mavis, can we see your map?"

I was so dumbfounded by all I'd heard that I simply pulled the map out and set it on the table. As LaKeemba unfolded the map, I could see hundreds of glowing dots all around the world.

"These are all magic people." I knew that without even thinking it.

"Yes, and they are all working, too. Just like you are. We all have our callings."

Jed giggled. "Ooh, a mission."

Sharon gave him a grim smile. "Today, your work has to do with the cabin, but we needed to get you here so that we could prepare you and the ship at the same time."

"Prepare us? Prepare us for what?" Unlike Jed, I was not looking forward to another mission.

"To save Capers. You're going to go back and save the town you're staying in."

"We're going to what? We can't do that. Changes in the past affect the future. It's a basic law of time travel. We can't do that." Jed was talking way too fast, and Sharon put a light hand over his.

"Breathe, Jed, breathe. We know the rules. Sometimes, rules need to be broken. This is one of those times."

Jed was shaking his head so hard that I was pretty sure he'd give himself a concussion if he didn't quit. "No, we just can't do that. I won't." He got up like he was going to storm out, but then he must have realized he was on a boat and sat back down again.

"We know the risks, Jed, but let us explain. You see, Capers has been in and out of existence for centuries. Most recently, it was there for three weeks in 2003, just long enough for the blackberry harvest and to gather a certain key that we needed. Before that, it had been forty-six years since the town had made it to the time period you live in," LaKeemba said.

Mr. Wilson gave his head a little shake as if to clear it. "Let me get this straight. The town where our cabin is comes and goes based on what has happened to it in the past. . . . Am I getting that right?"

"Yep, you got it." Shelby put down her pen. "But it's not really a simple thing to bring a town in and out. It takes something special." She looked at me and then down at the table.

"A map."

"Not just *a* map, Mavis. Your map. You're the map wielder, the woman who can twist time."

I was glad I was sitting down.

4

I t took me a while to make sense of what they were saying. I couldn't even wield a remote control effectively, much less a map. What was I supposed to do with a map? How was what I did with that map supposed to save a town? Why in the world would anyone pick me to be responsible for a whole town? There had been some kind of mistake.

But as I sipped my hot cocoa and let Shelby's words sink in, I knew there was no mistake here. This was the way of things. The people least prepared were often the ones asked to do the hardest things; that's what the pastor always said about Moses. And just look at what had happened the last time Jed and I had slid through time, and it had all worked out.

So here we were, sitting around a table and planning another adventure, this time one in which I would be responsible for the lives of hundreds of people. I knew I could refuse, that no one was forced to do this work—we'd learned that last time—but I also knew I'd regret the decision to refuse for the rest of my life if I took it. A map that let people time travel and a ship that flew were not the creations of people playing around. They existed for a reason, and apparently, I did too.

I poured the last third of my cocoa down my throat and placed both my palms flat on the table. "Okay, so what do we need to do?"

Every person looked at me, their faces blank as slates.

I stared from one set of eyes to the next, waiting . . . and then hoping . . . and then praying . . . until it became clear that no one had anything to say. I really wanted to go back to bed.

I took a deep breath. "Okay, so what's the threat?"

"President Roosevelt," Shelby said.

Jed spewed cocoa across the cabin. "The President of the United States is the dangerous one?"

"It's happened more times than we'd like to admit, Jed." Mr. Wilson's face was serious.

I swallowed hard and listened as Shelby explained that President Roosevelt had ruined the town, literally buried it in the forest, when he'd ordered the Shenandoah National Park and the Blue Ridge Parkway to be built. Now, we think of those things as good, she pointed out, but back then, a lot of people were really hurt, thought Roosevelt had "scammed" them as part of his bid for the presidency. I could hear the ire in her voice. I knew she could relate because she, too, had had something precious almost stolen from her by someone who was only out for himself. And I knew what I'd seen other, more recent, presidents do to win the Oval Office.

"So we're saving Capers from the creation of Shenandoah National Park? Doesn't that mean we'll be destroying the park?" Jed's question was a good one.

"Right. That park is beautiful, and tens of thousands of people visit it every year. Isn't the greater good most important here?" Mrs. Wilson was speaking very loudly. "I mean, I care about the people of Capers, but we can't save both, right? So don't we do the best good for the most people?"

She had a point, but something wasn't sitting right with me about that. Even though more people did enjoy the park because it existed, it felt wrong to say that Sunday drives and picnics were more valuable than people's homes.

"Mavis?" Alonso laid his hand on my arm. "You're the one who calls the shots here."

Great. I get to be the one to either doom a town and its community or to destroy one of the most beautiful things in a country. I put my head down on the ice table in front of me. It felt like an extreme version of flipping to the cool side of my pillow, and it soothed me while also giving me a minute to think.

LaKeemba spoke softly, "Few things in life are one or the other, Mavis. Find the third way."

I lifted my head slightly and looked at my friend. Her dread-locks framed her gentle face, and I could see light and softness in her eyes.

"A third way?" I sat up straighter then. "Yes, a third way. Maybe we can save them both."

"But the laws of time travel—" Jed was starting in again.

"I know what *Back to the Future* says, Jed, but maybe it's not totally right. Maybe we can find a timeline that keeps both Capers and the park." I was feeling heady with possibility now, even though I felt the knot of fear at the base of my throat still. "First, I think we need to scope out the town." I stood up. "Time to go to Capers."

Shelby, Alonso, Charlie, and LaKeemba stood up with me, but the Wilsons were slower to move. "I don't know, Mavis." The hesitation in Mr. Wilson's voice made me nervous.

But then, Jed stood up and said, "If Mavis thinks it can be done, I believe it too."

I felt the fear slide off my skin like a wet jacket. If Jed was in, we could do anything . . . at least I hoped so.

BACK UP ON THE DECK, Shelby took the wheel from Marcus. "Where and when to, Mavis?"

"Capers, um, when did the park open?"

"The historical society marker said the park was opened in 1926, but the first part of Skyline Drive didn't open until 1934." Mrs. Wilson had a keen memory for dates, which was good because my brain stored dates in a back, back, back room somewhere. "And Hoover built his camp up there in 1929, I believe."

"Alright, then, let's go to 1928, just to be sure we get there before things get wild."

Shelby gave me a nod and then turned the great wheel. "I'll point us in the right direction, Mavis, but I need you to get us to the right when."

I started to say that I had no idea how to do that, but then I felt the map twitch in my pocket. I took it out and unfurled it, holding tight to the paper in the wind across the ship's bow. The map was moving of its own accord now, trying to twist in my hand, and I almost lost my grip. But Jed grabbed one edge as I unfolded the paper all the way, and I saw, there on the top margin, the face of a woman. Her hair was long and streaming behind her in intricate braids, and her face was bold with a strong chin and a long, wide nose. The image looked like it was drawn with the same ink that had created the map, and the face moved. When she turned to look at me, I knew what I had to do.

"Hold tight, folks, we're off to 1928." I placed my cheek against the cheek of the woman on the page, and then we both closed our eyes. Behind my lids, I imagined a blue light like the one that had taken me to the cabin the night before, and I felt a gentle slide as if a spider web had draped across my face while I walked. When I opened my eyes, the ship was hovering just above the tops of tall trees, and the woman was gone from the map.

"Whoa, Mavis. That was awesome." Jed's face was wide with delight.

"Well, I guess it sort of was." I had no idea how I'd known to do that—it wasn't exactly normal to go cheek-to-cheek with a woman you'd just met, especially when she was part of a map. But it had worked. At least, I thought so. Something about the mountains around us felt like home. Maybe it was the gentle curve of them. Maybe it was that I recognized the kinds of trees. We were here.

Charlie asked me a question, and when I gave him a blank stare, he turned to LaKeemba. "Who was that woman in the map?" He looked a little smitten with his rosy cheeks and slim smile.

"Ah, that is Orisha Oyá, goddess of the wind. She is a mighty force, quick to help those who want to make good and big change. It was a great gift that she chose you, Mavis. She must believe you are capable."

I looked down at the map again. The place where Oyá had appeared was blank again, but I thought I could feel her there, just beneath the page, listening. "Thank you," I whispered.

"Now what?" Mr. Wilson looked a bit nervous as he peered over the deck into the trees.

"Now, we go down." I looked around. This ship was not going to make it into those trees, and I didn't think I was going to like our options.

"Marcus, can you help with the ladder?"

"Sure thing." The man stepped to the edge of the boat and flipped the same ladder we'd climbed up over the side of the ship. "All set." He grinned with a little mischief. Marcus knew I wasn't gifted with the Lord's good notion of physical grace.

When I looked over the side, I could see the ladder tapering down right into the trees. I looked up at Marcus. "Thank you," I said with a heavy dose of sarcasm, and he laughed. "You're welcome, Mavis. Have a good time." He squeezed my shoulders and then went back to the wheel.

"Who's first?" Alonso extended a hand to me as if to help me over the side and onto the ladder.

"Oh no, sir. I am not going to be taking my wide hips down that ladder until someone else"—I gave Jed a long look—"leads the way."

"I'll go." Mrs. Wilson was over the side before I had a chance to speak. A mother will do most anything to protect her son, I guess.

A minute or so later, Mrs. Wilson called from a long way down, "All set."

Jed followed her, and Charlie him. I went down next with Mr. Wilson just above me.

The climb was long, but I tried not to look down. As the ladder slid between the treetops, I saw the curved scallops of oak leaves and the thin arrowheads of beeches. I noticed, too, the long, arched leaves of a tree I didn't recognize, and when we got to the forest floor, Mr. Wilson said, "Did you see those chestnuts? They were massive. Gracious, what a loss that blight caused."

I remembered, then, that the historical society had talked about the chestnut trees that used to dominate this landscape and how a fungus had killed all the trees. "Ah, that's what those were. They were *huge*." I thought for a minute. "I wonder if we can save those, too."

Alonso took a leap off the ladder. "It's possible, Mavis, but perhaps it's best to concentrate on the work at hand rather than trying to do more and winding up doing less."

I nodded. There was such a thing as helping too much. I laid my hand against the bark of one of those massive chestnuts and felt him shift beneath me. I could only hope he understood.

WE WALKED a long way through the forest, following trails left by deer and other critters as we went. At first, I enjoyed the walk: the quiet, the beautiful trees, the tiny wildflowers peeking out in sunny patches.

But as the climb became steeper and went into its second hour, I began having visions of fainting and then being carried on a makeshift litter made from the men's shirts and small trees. At one moment, I even contemplated saying, "I'm not going to make it. Go on without me." I wasn't the world's most fit woman.

Just when I really thought I was going to have to call for a break, we stepped into a clearing on the crown of a mountain. The view from here was amazing—all valleys below and high peaks above—and I wasn't sure I had ever been in a more beautiful place. To our right, two thin strips of dirt carved by wagon wheels wandered off down the hill and back into the forest, and to our left, a cluster of buildings stood along the road and off a ways on smaller paths. I could see one building that looked larger than the rest. It stood two stories high, and a long, low porch stretched across the front. "The store," I said quietly.

"Not just the store. But the post office too." Alonso was speaking quietly right beside me. "One of these in most every town."

I looked over at my tall friend, and his face had this look of gentle awe and gratitude. He was a man who appreciated the places of history. That was evident in everything he did, but in this small town on the top of this small mountain, his appreciation turned to love, and it was written there in the soft lines of his cheeks and lips. I couldn't help but smile.

"That's Lillard's store. Been here since back before the war." A white man with a low cap and britches tied on with string came up beside us and stood looking out over the town too. "It's a good shop too. They never run out of flour or Boston Baked Beans."

Jed puckered up his face, and I gave him a look at the same time his mom said, "Jedidiah Wilson, you be kind."

The man turned to Jed and laughed. "Oh, not the kind of beans you're thinking of. It's candy. Peanuts coated in candy . . . don't know as they have them from when you come though."

I saw Mr. Wilson take a step back and then begin to inch forward again as if to step between this man and his son, but Jed put a hand on his dad's arm. "It's okay, Dad. He's one of us. I'm Jed Wilson."

The man pulled his hand out of his pocket and reached out to take Jed's. "I'm Slot McGee. Nice to meet ya. Nice to meet ya." I thought for a minute he might give Jed's shoulder a strain he was shaking his hand so hard, but then, he stepped back and smiled at me.

"It's good to see you, too, my lady."

I looked back over my shoulder to see if he was talking to Mrs. Wilson or Shelby or something, but no one was behind me. "Oh, well, thanks."

"Would you do me the honor of sharing your name?"

Charlie bumped into me from behind. "This is Mavis. She's wonderful. One of the best people I know."

I whipped my head over to Charlie and saw him grinning ear to ear. I began planning my revenge right then and there. Slot was at least thirty years younger than I was, and he looked like he hadn't eaten in about three weeks. Those two things alone meant we had nothing in common.

"I have no doubt of it, young sir. This fine woman here . . . she hasn't been seen nearly enough."

I spun around to look at Slot. "What did you say?"

"Oh, beg your pardon, my lady. I should explain. I can see what people were before they are what they are now. For some folks, that means I see what they used to do for a living, or sometimes, I see what people looked like as kids. Sometimes, it's pretty awful because I see what they were like before something awful happened, and then I have to see them as they are now. You, though . . . you I can see as a wisp, not really see you at all. I expect—and forgive me if I am wrong—that you were once an imaginary friend."

I was pretty sure my mouth was wide open for a few seconds until Charlie gave me a little hip check. "Um, yes, yes I was." My voice was very quiet, and I felt like I needed to sit down.

"Well, madam"—he scooped up my hand and kissed it—"while you are here in Capers, I plan to make it my mission to make you feel seen in every way."

I heard someone snicker, but when I turned to look at where the sound had come from, LaKeemba was standing rod-straight without a hint of a smile on her lips.

I felt Alonso sidle up beside me then and wrap an arm around my shoulder. I looked up at him, puzzled, but he just smiled gently and gave my shoulder a squeeze.

"Mr. McGee," Shelby said, "could you point us to the person in town that we should talk to about an important matter?"

Slot paused a moment, looked around at all of us, and said, "I can see how you have all been through something. I don't know that I really want to know what, but it seems like it might have to do with that ugliness that we've been feeling a while." He turned then and walked toward town. "Follow me."

I really wasn't much inclined to follow Slot anywhere—and what kind of name was Slot anyway? But it didn't seem as we had much choice. We had to find someone who might know more about what was going on.

Soon as we hit the edge of town, though, Jed said, "This town is full of magic folks."

"Sure is." Sharon gave a little shiver. "Lot of power here, folks. Lot of power."

"What does that mean?"

"Means whatever happens here only happens for one of two reasons." LaKeemba's voice was quiet but clear. "They let it happen, or someone makes them let it happen."

I remembered how Charlie's dad had made the HeavenLand folks do what he'd wanted them to do and felt a rock form in the bottom of my stomach.

As we walked into town, people came out on porches to watch us. No one looked threatening, which I was grateful for since several of the members of our group were black . . . in the South . . . in 1928. People looked mostly curious, and I figured that was because like calls to like, and everyone here knew most of us were like them, at least in the magic sense.

"There she be, friends," Slot said. "She'll be able to help you out. Mavis, I surely hope I have the pleasure of seeing you again." Then, he made this exaggerated bow and turned down the street. I felt Alonso's grip on my shoulder tighten just a bit.

When we reached the front of Lillard's store, a short white woman in a long skirt with her hair pulled back in a tight bun came out. "I'm Belinda Specker. Heard you might be wanting to talk." Her tone was matter-of-fact, no-nonsense. Not scary but not really that welcoming either.

"Yes, ma'am. I'm LaKeemba. We think we may be able to help . . . or at least we hope we will."

Belinda shook LaKeemba's hand. "We'll take all the help we can get. Ya'll come on in, and I'll get you a cold Pepsi."

Jed's Mom and I gave Jed a look. He was a die-hard Coke fan, and rudeness would not get us where we needed to go today.

We hadn't needed to worry, though. Jed took the glass bottle of Pepsi and thanked Ms. Specker for it as we all perched at the counter where the bins for rice and beans and sugar sat below us.

"Hercules send you?" Belinda said after we'd all gotten settled.

"You know Hercules?" Charlie's said.

"Don't nobody *not* know Hercules." Sharon sounded miffed, and I made a mental note to ask her about that later.

"Yes, Hercules brought us the trunk with the map," Mrs. Wilson said.

"A map, you say?" Belinda tilted her head and looked over at LaKeemba. "When was that?"

"2019," Jed said just as I was about to say, "Yesterday."

He had clearly given her the answer she'd been looking for because she looked at him when she said. "Ah, so we're working on a future situation."

I took a deep breath. "Well, sort of."

Belinda smiled, and the folds at the corners of her mouth softened her whole face. "Sort of pretty much the only way any of this works." She smiled and hoisted herself, long skirts and all, up onto the counter behind her, facing us. "I expect you all have seen that *Back to the Future* movie, haven't you? You're worried that you might erase someone from a photo like Marty McFly's family."

I heard Mr. Wilson chuckle before he said, "I see you're not one for abiding by that rule, if you'd seen that movie, I mean."

"No, sir. Don't abide by it at all. See, as I'm figuring, everything changes everything. If we can move through time like some people move through town, I expect someone has a finger on how to manage that, too. Besides, if we change something, might just as much be good as it would bad."

There was a sort of logic to Belinda's words, but I still didn't know if I wanted to be the one responsible for changing things.

"Tell me about this map." Belinda clapped her hands together like a child who'd just been told "they were happy and they knew it."

I started to pull the map out of my pocket, but for some reason, I decided to not show it around just yet. Maybe it was silly—Belinda seemed trustworthy enough—but I felt like Oyá wanted the map to be a quieter thing, not so flashy.

"It's a pretty straight-forward map," I said. "Kind of old-timey looking, but the special thing is that it lights up with where we're supposed to go next."

"And don't forget, it takes you there when you put your face near it, Mavis." Charlie wasn't always helpful. I had been planning on leaving that part out.

Belinda jumped off the counter. "What? The map moves you through time? You don't need the trees to do that?"

Most time travelers walked time by moving around 300-year-old trees, which was challenging in cities or places where most of the trees had been cut down. I could see why the map seemed exciting to her, and it was also why I had been thinking it wise to not share that little tidbit. If I found out there was a lot easier way to do something, I'd be tempted to get at it too.

"Can I see it?" There was a hint of ache in Belinda's voice.

Mrs. Wilson sat up a bit straighter at the counter. "Oh, we left it on the ship." She bumped my knee lightly. "For safekeeping, you know."

Belinda's face fell. "I see." She didn't sound happy.

LaKeemba stood then. "I expect it's about time for us to gather. Don't you agree, Belinda?"

The storekeeper had been staring at the floor, but at the sound of her name, she shook her head a little and looked up. "Gather. Yes, I suppose so. I'll ring the bell."

Back in HeavenLand, someone lit the fire, and everyone knew that was the sign to gather around. Here in Capers, they clanged a giant iron bell that hung on a post in front of the store. The building's porch made a sort of natural stage, and so when the townspeople came, LaKeemba only had to speak up to be heard by everyone.

"I expect you've heard by now that we are here because of the danger we've all been sensing for some time now. Some of us call it evil, and some of us just say it's The Shadow. But we all know it's been slowing us down, making our magic weaker."

Heads nodded in the crowd below.

"For a while, we thought it was just us, something brought on by the man who was hurting us back in our cown time. But now, now we think it's bigger, something more dangerous. Something affecting all the magic people."

There had been talk back at the farm about how The Shadow kept on coming. People talked about how their powers were hard to call forth, weaker sometimes. Jed told me that, from time to time, he thought he saw something dark and thick moving at the edge of his vision, but he never could get a good look at it.

For my part, I was finding it harder to become invisible. Shelby had suggested I practice my own magic so that it would come naturally when I needed it, and for a time, it had been getting easier. But then, it started to feel like I was wading through waist-high water anytime I tried. I kept on trying, but it was harder every time.

LaKeemba continued. "We don't know quite why we were brought here, but we know that part of our work is to help you save your town."

I looked out over the people below the porch, thinking they might be surprised to hear their town was in danger. But they were just nodding like they were grateful for the help that they already knew they needed. Once again, it felt like I was the last to figure things out. I slid my hand into my pocket and touched the map. She stirred beneath my fingertips, and I felt better, more sure I belonged.

"The rumors of the road that the president wants to put through here are true," Belinda spoke now. "We've expected it ever since they decided to make this parkland, and then when Roosevelt decided he was going to build that camp up here. . . . He saw it was beautiful and couldn't just let that beauty be as it was. He wanted to share it. . . Can't say as I blame him for that, except, well, sometimes the beauty needs to be kept quiet to stay beautiful."

Slot shouted, "And sometimes, folks get power hungry and want to be president and all."

I thought of all the coral reefs that were dying because of how many people scuba dived near them . . . and all the trash on Mt. Everest from the climbers. It seemed like us humans simply couldn't care for things if too many of us loved them or if we thought it was our right to take them for our own purposes.

Shelby stepped forward. "You know what to do. We just need you to tell us how we can help. How do we help save your town?"

The crowd started to murmur then, and I felt that niggling worry about changing the future come back again. Jed dropped his arm around my shoulder. "Marty McFly would not be happy," he said with a sad smirk.

No, no, he wouldn't.

JEDIDIAH

Mavis wasn't as worried about the whole "changing the future thing" as I was. It worried me something fierce. How could we save this town and also have that park that so many people loved? From what Dad had shown me on the regular map he found on the ice ship, Capers was right where the road would be built next year. It sure didn't seem like we could save it and still have Skyline Drive, and without Skyline Drive, the park wasn't the park.

I kept thinking about how maybe we could just get the road's path changed, but then, wouldn't that change other things, maybe even take out other towns. Saving the town and keeping the park just didn't seem possible.

But then, a few months ago, it hadn't seemed possible that I could walk through time . . . or that I'd find anybody else who had magical abilities, so . . .

While LaKeemba and Belinda talked with the crowd, I slipped off to the side of the porch and took the pencil and notebook out of my pocket. It was a thing I did now when I was nervous. I hadn't really known I could draw like I can until the HeavenLand folks came, but now that I *knew, it always made me feel better, more balanced maybe, when I did it.*

I started drawing the town then, the wide dirt road with the store on one side and a thin shed of a building that was, it looked like, the barbershop on the other. Just down a ways, there was a big, white house with a turret—like on a castle—and on further, more houses. Some of the houses were big and some barely shacks. A little gas station stood at the end of the row; it had some of those glass-topped gas pumps they always had on American Pickers.

I drew everything I saw with my eyes, and then I filled in the things that I saw the other way. I had never had been able to describe it well, this sight. I'd tried to tell Mom and Dad about it, Mavis, too, but all I could say was that I just saw things in my mind, things people didn't want most other folks knowing about. Sometimes the secrets were good —like that time Eliza was pregnant and just not saying anything yet— but mostly, what I saw was inky, grimy, the kind of things people didn't tell because they were covered in a black slime of shame.

Here in Capers, I saw some of those things—the man who lived in the third little house down who had a sort of black cat-like thing on his shoulder. It looked like it was whispering to him, and every time it leaned down, he shrunk back in the crowd a bit. He was afraid people would know about how he couldn't help himself but steal stuff. Or the woman whose arms were shriveled in my sight because she hit her kids all the time. That stuff was awful, but it had edges, ends. If something had an end, I could take it.

The other stuff, the stuff that puddled around everything—trees, edges of buildings, people's feet—that just kept spreading. I'd seen it first in HeavenLand, coming over from Poke's place, but then I had started noticing it around Roanoke, and then even once or twice up by the road at the farm. Here, though, here, it was everywhere. It wasn't quite reaching the center of town now where everybody was gathering, but it was moving. I could see it inching closer even as I sat there. I drew it, and I felt it turn toward me.

I dropped my pencil.

5

Nobody came to any consensus that afternoon. "Too many cooks," Shelby had said.

But LaKeemba told us she felt sure a plan would come together. I trusted LaKeemba, even if I wasn't sure I'd like the plan.

I was still uneasy about this whole idea of changing the past. Felt too much like we could lose something really good in the future, maybe actually make something really bad. So when we all gathered at the general store that night for dinner—Belinda lived upstairs and had a mighty fine kitchen in the back—I didn't feel much like talking. I ate my chicken and dumplings, thanked Belinda for the meal, and decided to turn in early. The family who lived in the big white house with the turret had offered us all a place to stay, and I figured if I settled in early, Sharon, my roommate for the night, wouldn't feel like she had to come and keep me company.

I had just about made a clean getaway when Alonso caught up to me on the front porch of the store. "Nice night for a walk. Want to join me?"

There was something about that man. Now, I wasn't crushing on him or anything like that. He wasn't my type, at least I didn't think so, but he had this presence about him, calm and assured. He just made me feel like it was all going to be okay. That night, I needed to feel like it would all be okay, so I took the arm he offered and walked beside him down the street.

We were quiet for a while, listening to the sounds of the summer bugs settle down into the trees on the mountainsides around town, but eventually, he said, "I've been thinking about something I'd like your figuring on."

I slid my eyes over and looked at him from the corner. "Is that so?"

"Yes, ma'am. I read recently that thirteen of the original colonies of the United States wouldn't have ratified the Articles of Confederation if slavery had been outlawed like some people wanted. The article claimed that it was worth slavery to form the United States . . . but I keep wondering what would have happened if they had just left those thirteen colonies to their own devices, let them go on their way and just formed a country with the people who agreed that slavery was too great an evil to let exist, especially in this new place designed for freedom."

I pondered that question a bit. No United States? But no slavery here either? It was a quandary for sure.

Alonso continued, "I mean, maybe we could have had something a lot better, a lot healthier, with a lot less painful history. Maybe we would have still had a United States of America, just a better version. Seems to me that it would have been worth trying that, that maybe what we have now isn't so great that it was worth all that pain."

I bristled just a little. I believed in the ideals of America, even if they weren't always lived out. The idea that the United States might not exist as I knew it . . . that took me a minute. Alonso left me time to think—that was something else I liked about him. He didn't fill the space with words. We kept walking around the edge of town.

The more I thought on it, the more I wondered if Alonso was onto something. What if the Founding Fathers had held out for the best? What if they had said no to the awful greed that drove people to makes slaves of other people and create the nastiness of racism we still lived with today? I couldn't help but feel a little sad that they hadn't tried.

We had stopped walking at a clearing in the trees just outside of town, and below us, the valley was a blue-green of dusk. I took a deep breath. "I see what you're doing here, sir."

Alonso grinned. "Is it working?"

"What you're suggesting is that maybe by changing the past for the people of Capers we might actually make a better future than the one we know."

He slipped my hand onto his arm and turned us back toward town. "It's possible."

As we walked back down Main Street, I looked around. Here, 181 people made their home. Belinda had been particularly proud of that number last night. Barbers and school teachers, mothers and uncles, children who hadn't even spoken their first word. I couldn't rightly decide that what I knew as the Shenandoah National Park, as much as I loved it, was worth risking their lives over, especially if we might just be able to save the town and make the Park better. I simply couldn't let the whims of science fiction time travel make me too scared to try to make something good for everybody.

Alonso gave me a kiss on the cheek before he went down the hall in the big white house to his own room. I swatted his arm and said, "Thank you, Alonso."

After I got into my pj's and climbed into bed, I pulled out the map. I still wasn't sure exactly why I was the one who could use it, but as weird as it felt, I trusted Hercules. If he knew I was the one, then I was . . . but the one what?

I MUST HAVE FALLEN asleep because I woke sometime in the dark of the night to hear Sharon softly snoring in the bed next to me. I felt around carefully for the map so that I could fold it up and be sure it didn't get damaged while we slept, but when I didn't find it, I assumed Sharon had taken care of it for me, and I drifted back to sleep.

The next morning, though, when I pushed my hair back from my eyes, I started. There, in the skin of my forearm, was Oyá's face staring up at me.

I laid gently back against my pillow and closed my eyes. *I must be dreaming. I'll just let myself drift deeper, and then when I wake up, it'll all be normal.*

I lay there a while, hoping to feel that lightening that comes as I drift off, but I felt wide awake. In fact, I felt so wide awake that I started to get antsy. I needed to pee, badly, but I couldn't bring myself to open my eyes.

Eventually, though, the need compelled me, and I lifted my head off my pillow, eyes still closed, and swung my feet over the side of the bed. Then, slowly, I drew my forearm in front of my stomach and opened my eyes.

She was still there, dark eyes trained on me. I sighed. Someday, I hoped I'd get used to the weird stuff, but today was not that day.

I stood up as gently as possible since I really didn't want to wake Sharon and have her see a woman staring out of my arm. I needed a few minutes to get used to my new tattoo before anyone else saw it.

Alas, I wasn't going to have a few minutes, though, because as soon as I got into the bathroom, I heard a voice. "Mavis, we need to talk." The voice was deep and sonorous, like if James Earl Jones were a woman. I love James Earl Jones, but there is no context in which the phrase "we need to talk" is going to be a fun conversation.

I let out a long breath and looked down. Oyá was looking at me again, but her face had softened. She looked sad, maybe. Or worried. Definitely worried . . . about me, I figured. "Mavis, you're in danger."

I dropped my head back and looked at the ceiling. "Again?" When I looked down at Oyá, she had a little smirk on her lips. "What! I'm in danger, you said. Why are you smiling?"

"Because now, woman, you have me."

"About that . . ."

"Oh, yes. The Map Keeper is charged with protecting the map at all costs. Every so often, I deem it best if the Keeper and I become one. . . . It makes it more difficult for errant hands to get to me. They'd have to kidnap you to get to me, and still, you'd have to—"

I groaned. "You do know I've been kidnapped once already, right?" I did not want to relive that experience again, not even for an orisha.

Oyá looked hard into my eyes. "I do know, Mavis. I also know that the experience brought you fully into your power. We will not wish for that to happen again, but if it should, we will hope for more magic to come to you." She smiled softly at me. "Agreed?"

I looked up at myself in the mirror and let invisibility wash over me before I smiled. "Agreed." I lowered the lid and sat down on the toilet. "You were saying something about how the map and I are in danger?"

"Yes, you and I are in grave danger, Mavis. We—"

"I'm sorry to interrupt again, but are you saying you're the map?"

"In a manner of speaking, yes. More accurately, it's like the map is my way of speaking to people some of the time. You can think of me as a bit like the Bible and the Holy Spirit all in one if it helps to consider me in terms of the tradition you best know."

I nodded. "But you're an Orisha, right?"

"I am."

"So, not Christian?"

"That's right. But not anti-Christian either. Just other. Just different. We call our supreme being Olodumare. Olodumare is all-powerful, all-knowing, just like your God."

"So Olodumare is God?"

"Sort of, Mavis. But different because we think of God differently."

I sat quietly for a moment and tried to wrap my head around this idea. Obviously, I had never been much for church, but the Wilsons went most Sundays. I guess I had absorbed some of what they'd been taught about one God, so I was struggling with this idea of other gods.

"Let me see if I can help, Mavis."

I looked down at her quickly. "You can read my thoughts."

"Of course," she said. "We are woven together for now, Mavis."

I let out a long breath. "Okay, help me understand."

"You've read those Percy Jackson books that Jed likes so much."

"Yes. I love me some Annabeth."

"Alright, so first, you know that Zeus and Artemis and the ten other major gods make up the Pantheon. They are the strongest, most powerful gods."

"Right. I'm with you."

"Then, you know there were other gods, like Pan and Prometheus, who had specific attributes and responsibilities in the world."

I nodded. I'd read every book Rick Riordan had ever written, so I knew my gods and goddesses of Greek, Roman, and even Egyptian history. "And there were nymphs and then gods like Thanatos who ruled over death. Sort of like levels of gods."

"Precisely. Olodumare is our highest level of God, and we Orishas are lesser gods, each with our own powers and responsibilities."

"I see. Okay, so what are your responsibilities and powers?" I felt a little embarrassed asking, like I should probably know this already.

Oyá smiled. "I am the goddess of the wind and change. I am responsible for clearing away that which has served its purpose, and I am a guardian for women." She had locked her eyes on mine, and I grinned.

"You protect women?"

"Protect. Empower. Fight for. Yes, that is part of my work." She was still looking at me, intently.

I let out a long shuddering breath and felt something give way inside of me, a barrier, a way I had been holding myself back out of fear that I was—even with my friends—alone. But I wasn't.

Oyá was here. As a tear slid down my face, I whispered, "Thank you."

"You are most welcome, Mavis. Always." Her face was soft and warm, but beneath that gaze, I now sensed an unwavering strength.

She turned her gaze ahead again. "To your original question, do you think that Percy and Annabeth and the other gods are somehow opposite of the Christian god?"

I laughed. "Of course not. They're made up."

Oyá smiled. "Are they? Maybe they were just another society's way of making sense of things that they couldn't understand as well as putting faces on a force or forces that seemed at work but could not be seen."

I pondered that a second. I had often wondered why so many people thought of God as "he." That didn't seem quite right to me somehow. I mean God had made all people, so weren't all people like God, not just half of us. I figured so many of us thought of God as "he" because our society taught us that men were the capable ones. I could see what Oyá was getting at—that we created God, or in her case gods, in our own image and in a way we could understand.

She nodded. "Right. So then, Olodumare and the Orishas are a way the Yoruba explain the world, the forces they can't explain or control. We are a place where people can place their trust. We give some measure of peace because we control what you cannot. We give you hope that it will all work out in the end but also the freedom that you don't have to work it out."

I liked that idea, liked that I didn't have to be responsible for everything working out. I let out of a long sigh.

"I am one face of that peace you feel, Mavis."

A tingle of relief flooded through me again.

"Good," she said, and I felt something steel within her. "We need to talk about how we protect ourselves."

"What are we protecting ourselves from, Oyá?"

"From Us."

IT TOOK ALMOST an hour for Oyá to help me understand the threat. By then, Sharon was stirring, and I figured it was time get going anyway. I slipped on a light sweater, grateful for the cool mountain morning, and headed to the general store. We'd all planned to meet up and discuss the plan over breakfast.

Sharon came in not long after I'd settled at the counter to eat the 1930s equivalent of a scone—some dry biscuit-like thing with raisins—and dropped to the stool beside me. "Heard you talking to yourself this morning. You alright?"

The wry lift in her tone told me that she knew full well I hadn't been talking to myself, so I pulled back my sleeve and let her get a good look at Oyá, who gave her a raised-eyebrow stare right back.

"Well, if that ain't something. Oyá, nice to meet you."

Oyá gave a gentle nod and then turned into profile as if she were looking toward the counter. Something about her expression told me she wasn't really seeing what I was seeing though. I shivered.

"Please don't tell everyone," I whispered to Sharon. "We are in danger, Oyá says. I'll explain that to everyone, but part of what will keep us safe is if people don't realize I am the map."

Sharon gave me a solid nod and didn't say another word, even though I thought I sounded like I had sustained a serious blow to the head.

Over the next few minutes, everyone else—Jed, Charlie, the Wilsons, LaKeemba, Shelby, Alonso, and finally Belinda and Slot—joined us at the counter with some of the strongest coffee in history and more biscuits, which became much better drizzled in honey, a lesson I learned by watching Belinda plate up her breakfast.

As everyone finished up their meals, LaKeemba jumped up to sit beside Belinda on the counter, much to Belinda's surprise, it seemed, and said, "Okay, so some of you seemed like you had reservations. How are you feeling about saving the town?"

So much had happened since I'd felt that way that I hardly remembered that as a worry, but I did manage to say, "I've come around. We should save Capers."

Alonso gave me a wink from down the counter, and I smiled.

"Good." LaKeemba scanned everyone seated there. "Anyone else have concerns?"

No one said a word, so she continued. "Okay, so then how do we do it?"

Jed spoke first. "I liked that man's idea that we see if we can't get them to allow for the town to remain in the confines of the park," he looked over at his dad, "but like Dad said, they can't let every town stay, so that's probably a slick slide."

Mr. Wilson laughed. "A slippery slope. Yes, I think Roosevelt and his people will shoot down that idea quickly."

"And they aren't going to move the park. Too much already invested in that," Slot said. "They been up here for months now measuring and marking trees. It's going where it's going."

Belinda nodded and said, "We're going to have to fight. Take on

Roosevelt and his people. I don't care." Her voice was shrill, and she was kicking her legs so hard against the counter I thought she was going to leave a mark.

The room got very quiet then, and it felt like we were stuck. Plus, Belinda's anger was distracting. It was hard to think when it seemed like we needed to calm her down.

Finally, I heard Charlie clear his throat. He had been very quiet since we got here, so I was a bit surprised to hear him speak up now. "What if we moved the town?"

Mrs. Wilson put her hand between his shoulder blades. "That's a nice thought, Charlie, but where would we move it? You can't just put a town anywhere. Besides, it's awfully hard to move buildings."

A heavy silence that felt like lead came into the room.

But Charlie wasn't done. "I think we could move it . . . in time, I mean." He took a deep breath. "I guess what I'm saying is that I think I could move it."

6

When kids say things, us adults are often really quick to dismiss them because we think either their ideas are naïve or too hard or just too simple. I could see the faces in that store gathering closed when Charlie made his suggestion.

But something about his words, the solid simpleness of them struck me, and I considered them. I felt Oyá shift beneath my sleeve, too, and a warmth of assurance passed up my arm to my neck.

"Tell us more, Charlie." I leaned forward so I could look the red-headed teen in the face. "How could you do that?"

He gave me a little smile. "Well, what if I could make it so time stilled here but moved around it . . . sort of like a rock in a stream. The park would be the new stream, and it would go forward just like it has always gone forward, just here in this spot, there'd be a pool of time that doesn't move."

Belinda dropped from the counter. "Are you saying you'd leave us stuck here in 1934?" She was angry.

Charlie's face flushed. "Oh, no, ma'am. Time would go forward same as always here . . . just at the edges, around town, there'd be a line, a place people after now couldn't cross into, almost like you weren't here. To them, you wouldn't be here. But for you all, it would be the same. The park would be there outside that boundary . . . but in here, the town would move along on its own."

LaKeemba leaned back and looked up at the tin ceiling. "So then people in the park from different times couldn't come in, correct? But you could set it up so people from in the town could go back and forth?"

Charlie nodded. "I think so. I mean, I've never done this before, but I think I could do it." He let out a hard breath. "Only thing is that the only other people who could come here besides the people in Capers when I made this pocket of time would be other time walkers. Otherwise, it won't work. At least, I don't think so."

I saw the other adults look at each other, doing that thing where they decide without the kids in the room, and I didn't like it. "If Charlie thinks he can do it, I say we let him try. What's the worst that can happen?"

Charlie looked down at this hands. "I could lose the town in time."

"Oh," I said.

Slot stood up. "Let's try it." Belinda gave him a look that could have stopped his heart if she'd had that power.

Charlie looked up at him. "Really? What if I mess it up?"

"We've got a time spinner here, too, Esther. Let's get the two of you together. I expect the two of ya'll can get it." Slot was on his way to the door already.

LaKeemba slid off the counter. "That's settled then. Charlie, get up with Esther and get working."

Belinda jumped off the counter and slammed the kitchen door on her way out.

We all stared at the door for a moment until LaKeemba spoke again. "Alonso, maybe you can be of some help, too?"

I thought maybe LaKeemba was giving Charlie a chaperone, but it turns out Esther was Ninety-three. . . . She and Charlie set to work right away, holing up in a corner of the store with a clock, a frog, and a bottle of birch beer, Esther's favorite. Alonso took a seat nearby, and from what I could see, he was working hard to do his thing and juice up their time-stopping ability. I expected him to be the most tired of them all when this was done and made a note to bring him a big cup of hot cocoa with lots of marshmallows when we got back to the farm.

Meanwhile, I had my own stuff to contend with, and I headed for the door. LaKeemba stopped me on my way out. "You know, Mavis. You saw her reaction, right?"

Belinda was part of the "us," Oyá had mentioned. I had thought that might be the case from the first conversation we had with her when she had seemed a little grumpy we were there. But now, it was clear. "I know."

LaKeemba gave me a sad look and nodded, and I went out the door.

I slipped back to our room, and when I slid out of my sweater, Oyá's gaze was turned forward again. I wanted to get her attention, but her expression made me shy. I sat and stared at her and then straight ahead as I thought about what to do. Then, something began to form before me, a wide gray, gathering like a cloud beyond my close vision.

As I watched, the gray looked like it was taking on a form—a person's form—and then, it turned toward me. But before its gazed reached mine, I felt Oyá jerk, and I looked down. "Don't look into its eyes, Mavis." Her voice was stern. "Recognition gives it power. . . . To be seen is, as you know, a gift."

I nodded. I did know, and I didn't want to give that thing, whatever it was, any power, not any at all. "What is that thing?"

"It does not go by a name . . . or maybe it would be more accurate to say we do not allow it to use its name. Names also carry power."

"Okay, but what is it? Some sort of evil spirit or something?"

"Sort of." Oyá looked off in the distance over my right shoulder. "We call it 'The Shadow.' It is the thing that is created when we divide ourselves."

I must have looked confused because she said, "Think of humanity as one being, one creation all linked. In the Christian tradition, you often hear talk of The Body, like the people in the church. When The Body gets divided from itself because people decide to separate from one another—maybe because of a disagreement or because of prejudice or even something simple like the way someone dresses—The Shadow gets stronger. So it tries to make people oppose one another."

"It's responsible for wars and stuff?"

"Oh no, humans do that. But it is responsible for entrenching those wars, making it seem impossible to overcome divisions."

I thought a minute and then said, "Let me see if I got this. Let's say I decided I wasn't going to like that guy across the street"—I pointed to a man patting down his brown and white horse outside the general store—"because he has pointy boots and I like square-toe boots. I'm creating the problem between us, but

The Shadow makes me believe that this man and I can't get along because we prefer different boots."

Oyá smiled. "Yes, Mavis. Exactly. I had no idea you felt so strongly about boots."

I started to tell her it was an example, but then I caught her grin. "Basically, The Shadow is getting really strong right now, huh, given how much we decide we can't be friends with people because of who they voted for or what religion they practice or where they grew up?"

"I have seen it stronger in times of world war. When Hitler came to power, The Shadow was mighty. So it's not as bad as it has been, but for a time when the world is a relatively peaceful place —at least in terms of military efforts—The Shadow is very, very strong. This worries me."

It worried me, too, but I had no idea what it had to do with me. I couldn't take on some awful thing that had been around forever. I was just one woman.

"You don't have to take on The Shadow, Mavis. It gets weaker the same way it gets stronger. When people come together, it's power lessens. The more people see beyond their differences, the more The Shadow fades into the background. Still, it's not your job to try to defeat it. Your job is to help save this town."

I let out a sigh of relief. "Charlie's got that one covered."

Oyá looked at me, sternly. "It is *your* job, Mavis, to help save this town. Charlie has his own part of the work to accomplish, but not all of it. You, too, must do your part."

I gritted my teeth. "But I don't know what in the dickens to do, Oyá. Care to enlighten me?" I was angry, and my tone showed it.

I felt my right arm begin to tingle and then to get very warm, almost hot. "Do not speak to me that way, woman. I have gifted you with my presence and my help. Do you disrespect me because you are frustrated?"

Color spread up my face. "I'm sorry, Oyá. You're right." I let out a shuddering breath. "I just don't know what to do."

As the warmth faded from my arm, Oyá tilted her head and looked at me. "You can do almost anything, Mavis, as long as you are working out of a place of love and clarity. Few things can go wrong with those two elements as guides."

I didn't feel clear at all. I felt like I was walking in a tunnel with my arms out in front of me. Any minute now, I might walk into a wall or step off a cliff or put my hand on a poisonous tunnel snake.

I felt Oyá shift, and a tiny relief from the tightness in my chest, a shift of the weight off my shoulders. "It is not yours to figure out all the steps, Mavis. Just the next one."

I let out a long sigh. I knew it should feel easier to figure out just the next step, but I still didn't know what that next step was. I stared a while into the tree-covered mountainsides beyond the town. If I didn't look closely, the hillside looked uniform, like it was covered in a blanket of green. But the more I stared, the more I could see the different shades of green and the various shapes of the different trees. Some were pointing straight up, some stretching wide. Still others had a scraggly arm reaching up and out from the rest. Their uniqueness was what made the mountainside beautiful.

As I stared, I felt that gentle gathering of an idea coming together, and the firmer it got in my mind, the more I felt Oyá's smile under my skin.

A LITTLE WHILE LATER, I had a full plan—or at least the first part of a plan—and I was headed out of the room to tell everyone at the store. Oyá stopped me though. "Mavis, first, look at your left arm."

I peered down, and there, woven amidst my skin, were the outlines of the world's continents. "The rest of the map," I said as I looked over at Oyá on my other arm. "Has it been there all along?"

"Yes, but you didn't need it then. You do now."

I stared back to my left arm, and I could see a faint glow of gold in the Virginia mountains, marking where we were here in Capers. Then, I felt a cold pulse, like someone had tapped the underside of my wrist with an ice cube. When I turned my arm over, there, right in the upper third of the African continent, just a bit west of center, I saw a blue pulse.

"I don't know my African countries very well, Oyá."

"Nigeria, Mavis. You need to go to Nigeria."

"Okay, well, I don't know anything about Nigeria. What should I know?"

"We don't have time to correct the oversights of your education, Mavis, but I'll be there to guide you. We must go now."

I didn't like the idea of slipping off in time and space without telling anyone where I was headed. I realized this was odd, of course, since most of my existence I'd never had anyone know I was anywhere, but once people care about you, it starts to matter that they can care for you well.

"Jed will know, Mavis. Not when or where, but why. We must go now, Mavis." She was looking out in the distance again, and I wondered if she was seeing The Shadow.

"Okay, like this?" I wrapped my fingers around my wrist, placing my thumb on the gold glow and my middle finger on the pulsing blue light . . . and just like that, I was in the middle of a desert, and I could see a line of soft-peaked mountains in the distance.

"Welcome to Yorubaland, Mavis. Home of my people."

I took a deep breath and began to walk toward the mountains.

JEDIDIAH

I felt Mavis go the instant she time walked. It wasn't a shock or anything. More like a loss, kind of like when you know someone has walked out of the room. "Mavis had to go," I said to Mom and Dad.

"Go? Go where? By herself?"

"She has someone with her." I felt sure of that, even though I had no idea who that someone was. Still, I was sure.

I was even more sure that their going had to do with Capers but also with the bigger evil shadow of the puddle-thing I'd seen creeping around us ever since that first visit to HeavenLand. I trusted Mavis, knew she wouldn't leave if she didn't need to. But I still worried. I could tell from Mom and Dad's faces that they were worried too.

"Okay, then. Well, Mavis can take care of herself." Dad's voice was confident, but I saw him shoot Mom a concerned look.

"She can, Dad. She'll be fine. Right now, we need to see if we can help Charlie." Ever since Charlie and Esther had started working, I'd been seeing that puddle of darkness getting closer and closer to the store. Now, it was coming right to the door.

I stood up from the counter. We'd been sipping Pepsi from glass bottles that had come out of one of those old machines that Mom was always looking for in antique stores so she could "pay for my education," but I headed to stand behind Charlie, facing the door. Mom and Dad flanked me on either side, and I giggled as I pictured them putting their hands up in fists in front of their chests. They were ready.

Earlier that morning, I'd finally told them what I'd been seeing; it was too scary for me to keep it to myself anymore. I knew the folks from HeavenLand could sense it coming, and I expected the magic people from here in Capers did too. But no one else, as far as I knew, could actually see the oily spread of shadow coming in. I was so terrified, and somehow, having Mom and Dad know that helped, like I'd handed them a tiny bit of it to carry for me.

As we stood between Charlie's back and the store door, Alonso stood from his chair beside Esther and faced outward too. Then, I saw LaKeemba and Shelby come from the back room and take their stands on the other two sides of the table. We'd formed a protective circle around Charlie and Esther. I hoped it would be enough.

"Thank you," I heard Charlie whisper. Then, the door began to shake.

7

At first, it seemed like the mountains were close. *We'll be there in an hour or so,* I thought, which was a good thing because it was so hot. I'd already shed my sweater, and then I'd ripped off the bottom half of each pant leg by starting a hole in each knee on a rock. Finally, I'd done what I'd sworn I'd never do—I tucked my shirt up into itself and exposed my belly. I knew I was risking not only a very nasty sunburn but sheer embarrassment if we met anyone here in the desert—rather unlikely. But I didn't care. I was *so* hot.

Oyá kept me from taking off my tennis shoes only with some choice words about what the bite of a viper would do to my flesh. Her words made it feel like my feet were going to melt off my body . . . but I kept going. I wasn't sure what I needed at that mountain, but I knew I needed it. What I didn't know was why the blasted map hadn't dropped me off closer to it.

Still, Oyá was good company, and while we walked, she told me about Yorubaland and her people. She talked of their wealth, about the villages and customs that had existed there throughout history. She told me that Yoruba people had more twins than anyone in the world and that she had special charge over these babies. When she spoke of them, a sweetness crossed her face, and I wondered, for a minute, if tenderness was just the underside of strength.

Finally, after what felt like a lifetime, we reached the foot of the great stone mountain that Oyá told me was called Idanre. It looked like water was pouring down its side, almost like tears, and I instantly loved that a rock could cry. Around us were other mountains, rounded stones that towered above us. We stood in a low valley that reminded me of the hollows of the Blue Ridge, and I felt at home.

"In your time, Mavis, a town is here. But we came here, to this time, for a reason."

I looked up at the mountain and thought I saw a figure moving. "Is someone up there?"

"Hold on," Oyá said, and before I even had time to say "Hold on to what?" a gust of wind lifted me off the ground and up into the sky.

A second later, I was standing at the top of Idanre, and there, smiling, was Sharon. "Hi, Mavis. About time you got here." She grinned and gave me a hug.

"Wait! What! How did you get here?"

"Another time, Mavis." Sharon turned me so I could look out over the valley below. "What do you see?"

I gazed out over the valley and into the distance. "It's beautiful."

"Yes, it is. But see more than the beauty, Mavis. Look, woman."

I turned first left and then right, and then I glanced down at Oyá, and she nodded. "It's almost completely protected by the mountains. The valley, I mean. It's like a fortress in here."

Sharon smiled. "That's it." She turned to face me.

"What? We're supposed to move Capers here."

I felt a pinch in my right arm. "No, Mavis. We don't take other people's land even if it helps us. Too much of that has happened already. No, Capers won't be moving here." Oyá's voice was hard and brittle. She was angry.

The question seemed reasonable to me. We had people who needed a new home, a place to start over, and here was a perfect place.

Sharon put a hand on my cheek. "Helping people doesn't always have to hurt other people."

I looked down at the valley. Oyá had said there was going to be a town here someday. So if we put Capers here, then that town might not come at all . . . or if it did, it wouldn't be the town it was supposed to become. I let out a sigh. All this trying to do the right thing was complicated. I guessed I just had to hope it would work for Charlie to keep the town where it was. "Then I don't understand. Why are we here?"

"To learn, Mavis." Sharon didn't sound annoyed, which was good. But she did sound sad.

"Okay," I said. I stared down at the valley again. I studied the hillsides, the way they formed little valleys. Back home, each of those would be a stream, and there'd probably be a river at the bottom . . . and that river would empty out of a hollow . . . "That's it, isn't it? We need to build a town in a hollow so that it's protected and we only have one place to defend."

Sharon dropped her arm around my shoulder and bumped my hip with her own. "Not just for Capers. For us."

"For the magic people." I felt it then, the way something settled into place in my mind, behind my ribs, too. Here was our answer to The Shadow, a place to take a stand. "Alright, I got it." I wrapped my arm around Sharon's waist and looked down at Oyá. "Thank you."

Then, I stood up straight. "We best be getting back then." I was eager to tell Jed the plan.

"Not quite yet." Sharon looked to my right, and I saw a woman in a bright-yellow dress coming toward me. On her head, she had a hat, or maybe a scarf, that spanned out from her head like sunbeams. She looked amazing—beautiful but also powerful and strong as well as something I longed to be: confident.

"This is Adesina. She is your guide for today," Oyá's voice was soft. "Attend to her, Mavis. Attend well." Then Oyá slid back, almost invisible in my skin.

"Greetings," Adesina said as she approached. "Oh, nice kicks. Jordan 20s, right?"

I smiled at her then down at my shoes. "Yes. You know shoes? I only know that's what they are because Lizzie insisted I know that these are classics now."

"Well, for us, when really is 'now,' huh?" Adesina laughed. "But enough talk about shoes; we have a path to make."

I had no idea what she was talking about, but if Sharon and Oyá had brought this woman, I knew to trust her. "Okay!"

She turned then and looked out over the hill. . . . I saw her wave her open left hand, palm down, across the air in front of her, like she were caressing the tops of the mountains. Then, she moved her hand back to just right of the center of her body and pointed her index finger. "There."

I looked in the direction she was pointing and saw, if I didn't try too hard to see it, a shimmer that looked like a road across the air, winding off into the distance. "That's our way, then?"

Sharon and Adesina nodded. "Do we just walk out on it?" I started to take a step forward.

Sharon grabbed my arm and shouted, "No, woman. You can't walk in the air!"

I looked at her with surprise and then a little bit of frustration. "Seriously, this is where we draw the line. We can travel through time. We can light fire with our fingers. We can carry goddesses in our skin, but we can't walk in the air."

Sharon laughed hard and bent double. "You got a point, Mavis. You got a point. No, *you* can't walk in the air. Some of us can, though." She looked over at Adesina.

"I'll see you there." Then, Adesina stepped out off the mountain onto the shimmering road.

I had seen a lot of amazing things in the past few months, but nothing could top a regal woman clad in golden light, walking through the sky.

After a few moments, Sharon said, "Okay, we need to get going too." She headed toward a wide path that I could now see, carved in the hillside.

I scuttled after her, wishing I could be as graceful as Adesina. "Where are we going?"

"You tell me. You carry the map." She tossed a smile over her shoulder.

I looked down at my rapidly-reddening left arm and saw the map there. Now, though, Africa was facing me, and two golden dots were pulsing right where we stood. I turned my arm over, and there, the blue dot was just northwest of us.

I gave Sharon a nod, and she threaded her arm through mine. I encircled my wrist, and off we went.

. . .

WE ARRIVED in a busy market full of stalls with people selling everything from spices to sweaters. The sound of car horns and machinery told me we'd come closer to my home time, but how close, I couldn't be sure. The market had an old-world feel to it, like it were operating on rules and practices set up long before any of us had been alive.

Sharon and I walked through the stalls and looked at beautiful lamps made of silver and brightly-colored glass, and I tried to look around and see what might tell me where and when we were. It was a habit I'd begun cultivating from the first time walk that Jed and I had taken to Moscow, and I sort of enjoyed the puzzle of it. Most of the vendors were men, although I did see a few women cooking in the back of a few booths. All of the women I saw, except for Sharon and I, were wearing long-sleeved, loose-fitting shirts that extended down to mid-calf and pants that reached their ankles. Most of the women also had scarves on their heads, and a few had veils over their faces too. I knew enough to realize we were in a Muslim area but probably not one of the communities that had very strict dress codes for women. None of these women were in burkas. TV had taught me a lot.

Eventually, Sharon and I made our way out of the market and into the streets of the town. I didn't really know where I was going, but it felt like—in this new sense of direction that had come since the map had arrived—we were headed in the right direction. Eventually, we wandered onto a winding street and into a wide plaza. I led us to the edge of the open park-like space and down a small street, and there, shimmering like a gemstone, was water.

I had not been expecting that even though when I looked down, I did see that our golden dots were right next to a body of water.

"You found it. Welcome to Al Hoceima, Morocco," Adesina said from just behind us.

I did a double take. "How did you get here so fast by walking?" I immediately felt dumb for asking. If the woman could walk in the sky, then surely speed was not an issue.

She smiled but then frowned when she saw my face. I was confused. Very confused.

"I thought you were making a way for us, but I used the map to get us here." I sounded like a whiny second grader, but I couldn't help it.

Adesina nodded and then pointed toward a low wall around the plaza behind us. "Let's sit."

As we looked over the plaza, I saw young children running and chasing one another and parents watching carefully but letting them have their fun, too. I smiled.

"I make ways, Mavis. But they're not all roads. Sometimes, I have to clear some stuff out. That's what I did this time."

I looked at her carefully and then looked back across the plaza. "The Shadow."

"Yes. It's growing stronger."

I sort of knew that. I couldn't have said how, but I did. "So we had to come here before going back to Capers? We can't make that trip directly now, can we?"

Sharon leaned back and put her hands on the wall behind her. "No, we can't, but fortunately, I think our ride is here."

I glanced back toward the sea, and there, shining, was our ship with Marcus at the wheel. I stood up. "Time to go!"

8

The ship ride from Al Hoceima to Capers took only a few hours. I got the sense that we could have been there much faster but that Marcus had slowed us down to allow us to rest and prepare a bit.

Adesina and Sharon spent most of their time in the cabin with me playing cards or taking naps, but every so often, one of them would go up to the deck. I assumed they were checking on Marcus and evaluating the path we were traveling, but honestly, I didn't have the energy to care just then. I needed to rest, to give my brain time to catch up to what was happening. So when I was alone, I just kept dealing myself hands of solitaire and piling up the cards. Sometimes, the best downtime is something that distracts your mind just enough that the rest of your brain can do some work for you.

I kept thinking about what Oyá had said, about The Shadow, about how it fed on division and strife. Mrs. Wilson talked a lot about how ugly people were to folks who didn't agree with them on Facebook, and the more she talked, the more I was glad I didn't have an account. It sounded mostly like a place where people fought.

I could see that same tension in our neighborhood though. An election was coming in November, and the candidate signs had begun to show up in June. Then, as November got closer, the signs got bigger and more numerous. One pair of houses next to each other looked like they were in a competition to see whose political signs could be the biggest. Their yards looked like Times Square without all the flashing lights.

All that's to say, The Shadow had plenty to feed on just now. Plenty of division. Plenty of strife. And I had no idea what I was supposed to do to fight that. Just the idea of fighting it felt like it would make things worse. I mean, telling people they needed to be kinder to each other seemed like a sure way to make people dislike me rather than make them like each other.

I dealt another hand of solitaire. As I pulled the ace of hearts off the deck and laid it over my columns, I felt Oyá stir. She'd been very quiet, and it felt like she had been praying or something. I don't know how I knew that. It just felt like she—we—were reaching into something bigger, something that was giving us strength and even a smidgen of peace. My chest felt a little less tight.

"Mavis, woman, listen." Oyá's voice was quiet, sonorous, like a deep bell. "We cannot fix the world. That is beyond our work."

I remembered our conversation about Olodumare earlier and nodded.

"In fact, we can't fix much of anything, sometimes even ourselves. But we can try to make amends, to tend peace, to—as your Bible says—'live at peace with everyone.'"

I felt a little uneasy with that, like she was suggesting I be a doormat, let people walk all over me.

"No, Mavis, this isn't about cowering or hiding the truth for fear of disagreement. And this isn't about you shrinking or becoming less of yourself. This is about speaking truth but in love. Reminding ourselves and others that we are all doing the best we can with what we know and who we are, challenging ourselves and others to do better but giving space for grace also."

Oyá was using language I knew, words that would sound familiar from my time at church with the Wilsons. I was grateful that she put forth the effort to help me understand, but I also remembered Shelby telling me how tired she got of having to help people understand things all the time. Shelby had been talking about racism, but it seemed like Oyá was doing the same kind of thing here . . . but then Oyá was a goddess, so maybe she didn't get tired.

"This a great, small work, Mavis."

That was an oxymoron if ever I heard one.

Oyá laughed. "Yes, it is a paradox. The small things we do have great impact. Mend a relationship with someone you know, and it may ripple out into every relationship each of you has."

I felt the ring of truth there. I also felt very tired. This seemed like really hard work.

"'Only the thing for which you have struggled will last.' That's a saying of my people. We have a challenge ahead, but it is a challenge we can manage together. It is about people you love, Mavis, and that challenge is always worth struggling in."

I knew that to be true, too. I would do anything for Jed, for the Wilsons, for my friends from HeavenLand, even for Charlie. Just thinking that made me feel stronger.

"Good. You are ready. You must begin the work in Capers, Mavis. Remember our plan." Then, she paused and looked up past my head. "We are here."

I stood and looked out the window behind me and saw the trees of the Blue Ridge swaying below me. I took a deep breath and headed up on deck.

I'D LIKE to say that climbing down the ladder was less terrifying this time, but I don't want to lie. There is just something not right about a wide-hipped woman climbing a rope ladder out of the sky. Okay, maybe there are a lot of things not right about that, starting with "ladder out of the sky."

When I reached the ground, I did my best slow jog into town and stopped dead in my tracks when I saw the buildings of Capers. They were all shrouded in what appeared to be a charcoal-gray cloud. Puddle? Sometimes it seemed like vapor, sometimes like ooze . . . in any case, I could barely see the town through it.

I took a deep breath and peeked down at Oyá. She was staring straight ahead with me, and a gentle golden glow was emanating from her face. Beside me, I felt Sharon, Adesina, and Marcus straighten up. Then, we walked into The Shadow.

As we moved forward, the gray slid back, not far, but away enough that the air began to feel lighter. I looked back, thinking I'd see we were enclosed, but the path we'd walked glowed bright and clear in the late afternoon sun.

I felt Oyá's glow grow stronger the closer we got to the general store, and Sharon took my hand. With each of our steps, The Shadow slid back more, and soon, we were walking up the porch steps and opening the door of the store.

At first glance, everything seemed just as we'd left it, more or less. The counter, the shelves stocked with things, our friends inside together. But when I looked at Jed's face, I knew nothing was normal.

"Mavis!" I saw him start to run toward me but then stop with a glance over his shoulder at Charlie. "You're back." He almost groaned the words, and I could hear the fatigue in his voice.

"We're back, and we're ready, Jed. You're not alone. None of you are," I said, and I was surprised by how much like LaKeemba I sounded. I liked it. "We have a plan."

I scoured the room for Belinda so that I could ask her to call the townspeople in to begin the work, but it took me a while to find her. I finally saw her behind the counter. I had missed her at first because she was obscured by gray, still surrounded by The Shadow. I started to rush over but felt Oyá resist and then Sharon grab me by the arm.

"No, Mavis," Sharon said. "She has made a choice."

I looked more closely at the town leader, this strong woman, and I could see it in her face, too, there behind the fog. She was determined, resolute, and angry.

"Yes, I have made a choice. I'm done tired of my people getting stomped on because we don't live in the big city or have that big city education. Ya'll outsiders think we can't take care of our own here in Capers, but we can. We don't need ya'll. So get out." She took a step forward, and The Shadow around her grew.

I glanced at Jed, and for the first time, I noticed that our friends were circling the table. Alonso gave me a small nod. "You stay, okay? Protect Charlie and Esther," I said. "We've got the rest." Then I moved slowly toward Belinda, Sharon's hand in mine again.

"Belinda, we don't want you to get stomped on. That's why we're here. You're right. We don't think you all can do this without help, but it's not because we think you're helpless. It's just because we know how much we need help sometimes." I was talking, but I wasn't really thinking much about what I was saying. Mostly, I was just hoping that The Shadow didn't grab me or swallow me or make me hate my friends.

Belinda tilted her head to the right just a little, and The Shadow grew a little thinner, just for a minute. But then, she furrowed her brow, and the gray thickened even more. "Nope. I've heard that before. That's what Roosevelt said when he came up here and built that school." I remembered that the historical society folks had told us about Roosevelt building a school up here in the mountains only to then force all the families of the children who went there out of their homes. "Now, I know he was just scouting his stupid park and that road that'll come through our town. He pretended to want to give us something only so he could take."

I knew what she meant. I could see how what the president had done felt conniving. I didn't know if it was, didn't know if that had been his intent. But intent didn't matter when people got hurt.

I started to tell Belinda I understood, started to commiserate, but Belinda put up a stiff arm in front of herself. The Shadow puffed out, almost to us, and I felt Oyá's light get stronger, wrapping us more deeply in her power.

"No, you won't fool me again. We're going to do this our way or no way. So you all best be moving along."

I felt like she had been going to say "before I make you," but instead, she walked out the front door of the store.

LaKeemba and Marcus looked at me, and I nodded. I didn't know how I'd become the one in charge, but I was, and there was no time for me to second-guess myself. "Stay together." Then, they walked out the door after her.

I turned back to the table and finally had a chance to see what Charlie and Esther were doing. There, centered between them, was a tiny replica of the village. At first, I thought it was something Jed had created from twigs—like he'd used to do when he was overwhelmed and needed to do something with his body but couldn't ride his bike—but as I got closer, I could see it was an image, like a movie.

It was alive.

There, on the street that I'd come in from a few minutes ago, I saw people walking around. A person in a wide-brimmed hat stepped into the barbershop. Another hung sheets on a line outside her house. Slot sat outside the store on the front porch, a cigar between his lips. This *was* Capers. "Whoa," I whispered. I almost didn't notice The Shadow because I was so amazed at the mini town, but it was still there, faded a bit, like the clearing of smoke after a fire, but still very much there weaving in and out amongst the buildings.

Alonso leaned over to my ear and said, "It's two minutes from now. The whole town, just a bit ahead." I must have looked puzzled because he nodded toward the door and said, "Go see."

I stepped outside the store and looked around. I saw Slot there on the porch right away and only ducked back in the door just in time to avoid another awkward conversation with the man. In a few seconds, I watched from the doorway as the man with the wide-brimmed hat walked into the barbershop and a hand draped a bright white sheet over a line.

Then, careful not to get Slot's attention, I scoped the town for Belinda and tried to will The Shadow away even more. I didn't know how that worked, how we made ugliness fade, but it felt like the gray lifted even a tiny bit more as I hoped it would. Maybe hope was enough for a little while.

Then, I saw a darker pocket down the road a bit, and a small crowd of people was gathering. Belinda was making her move, and I didn't like the looks of it.

I hustled back to the table to tell everyone what I'd seen but stopped cold just inside the door. There, in the air, hung Capers, like a baby's mobile suspended a few feet above the floor. As I watched, Charlie and Esther stood, and the tiny floating version of the town began to grow. Slowly the edges of it stretched out, and as it did, the group that had been guarding it stretched too. I heard LaKeemba and Marcus come in beside me, and we took each other's hands. Then, Mr. Wilson let go of Alonso's hand briefly to take mine.

As the town of two minutes ahead continued to expand and lay itself over the town of now, I felt a pressure against the back of my body, and I looked down to see The Shadow trying to creep in. I pushed against it and felt Oyá's power surge down my arm and into Marcus and LaKeemba then on around the circle of linked hands. As we pushed back against The Shadow, the town lifted up and over us, stretching still.

The Shadow was wheedling, trying to eek its way into our space, but I could feel the open air of our ring moving outward, making room for the future town, pushing back The Shadow. It must have felt it too because it got violent then, thrashing, battering against us. I felt like someone was hitting me in the back of the head with a heavy book.

I tightened my grasp on LaKeemba's and Marcus's hands and saw Oyá looking straight-ahead, her jaw set hard. I took a long deep breath and then pushed out again, Oyá's strength coming up to lift mine. The battering stopped. A lightness came in behind us. The Shadow had retreated. I could still feel it back there at the edges of the wood, and down the road, a swath of it was still mighty where Belinda and her people stood. But we had done it. We had saved Capers. Or at least I hoped we had.

We got Esther home and settled into her favorite rocker on her front porch with a cup of tea. She was asleep, head back and mouth gaping before we even got down her steps. Then, we celebrated for just a little while. We got Charlie a huge hot chocolate and took up rockers of our own on the store's front porch. Marcus had returned to the ship to be sure she was holding up with only twelve hours left of her life, but the rest of us sat and took a well-deserved rest.

It felt a little odd, sitting on Belinda's porch, her being against us and all. But the store was the center of the town, and it felt important to be a presence, to show confidence to the townspeople. Maybe to comfort ourselves too.

"Things fall apart. The center cannot hold. Mere anarchy is loosed upon the world." LaKeemba's voice echoed down the street.

"That's that Irish poet, right?" Jed had always understood poetry. At eight, he could recite the whole Jabberwocky poem from *Alice in Wonderland*.

"Right, Yeats." She smiled at him. "I'm glad you know that. The poem feels accurate for this moment."

Jed gave a solemn nod. "I wonder what rough beast is slouching toward us just now."

I had no idea what he was talking about, but LaKeemba's smiled widened. "Let's hope it's a good one and not that cloud of ugliness over there." She tilted her head slightly toward the edge of town where Belinda's gathering of The Shadow could be seen just over the top of the buildings.

We all grew quiet. This wasn't over. Not at all.

JEDIDIAH

When everyone headed back to their rooms to get some rest, I didn't feel much like napping. I stayed up on the porch and got out my paper and pencils again. I couldn't shake that image of a slouching beast from that poem LaKeemba had quoted. Our English teacher had said it was shaped like a Sphinx—person's head and lion's body—and so I started to draw it . . . all lean and golden as it crept across the sand. Its belly almost touched the ground, and its soft paws didn't make any sound.

As I continued to draw, the sand turned to a slope of a hill I knew was green, even if my pencils were just the grays of lead. Then, the Sphinx started moving up through the trees, and eventually, he walked—on the paper—right down Main Street.

When I looked up, they were there, in the middle of the street, but not a Sphinx . . . a person. Well, I say they were a person, but they were more than that. They took up a lot more space than one person. I could almost feel their skin against mine, and they were all the way out in the road.

"Jedidiah." Their voice sounded in my head like a drum. "You called me. I came."

I stood up and tried not to stare, but their face was so beautiful, like a lake I saw once high up in the mountains. So still it reflected everything around it but deep, too, deeper than I had ever seen. Their skin was deep brown and smooth like the bark of a beech after a rainstorm, and their head was bald, completely hairless. I felt like my words would fall short of even reaching them.

But I had to try. "Thank you. I hadn't realized I'd called you. I'm sor—"

They cut me off. "Don't apologize. Anyone who calls has need. I will help."

I let out of a hard breath of relief. "Thank you. We need it."

Then, this god—for they could only be a god—sat beside me on the steps and listened while I told them what they already knew.

9

I woke from my nap feeling groggy but better. I had the sense, as I splashed cold water on my face, that Sharon felt the same, Oyá too. All three of us were very quiet there in that small bedroom, but the weight of fatigue that we'd carried in didn't feel quite so heavy anymore. Sometimes, a nap is the very best thing, better than even doing something good.

But we also knew we needed to move. Capers was safe now, at least as best we could tell without going into the future to confirm, and we only had eight hours left with the ship. We had to trust that Charlie and Esther had done their work well because now we had to keep Belinda from undoing it.

I could feel myself getting angry at her, frustrated that she was so frustrated, but then I remembered what it was like for me to be invisible, unseen by most everyone. It was a horrible sensation, one I wouldn't wish for anyone else. I expected that's how Belinda felt. Invisible and tricked. After all, it did seem a little like the president had gotten to know the town only to gain the upper hand on them, kind of like Poke with the folks in Heaven-Land. It was skeezy, and I didn't like it.

I got it. I understood why she didn't trust us. What I didn't understand was why she'd trust The Shadow. As I pulled a brush through my curly hair and admired how the mountain air took away the usual frizz of summer, I tried to imagine what it would take for me to trust someone so awful. Then, I remembered hearing the writer Billy Coffey say at a gathering the Wilsons had that "When you're hungry enough, even poison tastes sweet," and I imagined Belinda was ready to eat anything that promised she and her town would be respected . . . whatever the cost.

Oyá stirred, and I looked down. Her eyes were sad. "It's time, Mavis."

I shoved the air out of my lungs and headed toward the bedroom door. I didn't want to do this, not any of it. I wanted to go back to the Wilsons' and enjoy my friends, time walk to pretty places, and eat Cool Ranch Doritos. But I knew I needed to do this, that my map was, somehow, a key part of our way forward.

It felt like Oyá squeezed my arm. "Don't worry, Mavis. We have help."

I didn't know what she meant, but I hoped she was right.

IT DIDN'T TAKE LONG for me to see the help Oyá had mentioned. As soon as I stepped out of the house and into the dirt roadway, I saw them, sitting next to Jed like they were old friends. But of course, the power and peace pulsing from them weren't what I felt from one of Jed's school friends. They were beautiful, beautiful and terrifying.

As we approached the general store, I kept my head down out of some sort instinctual reverence. I assumed this feeling came from Oyá because reverent isn't exactly an adjective most people would use to describe me. Clumsy, yes. Reverent, a big ole no.

But Tat that moment, it felt right to bow somehow, and as I took what felt to be the three-mile walk across the road, I wondered why I'd never felt this way when I went to church with the Wilsons. Surely, if I were walking into God's house, I should feel the same way. But there, I was always worried about whether I'd dressed right or if I'd sing okay. And a lot of the time, I was wondering if the pastor was going to say something that made me mad—like how America is a special nation. *Exceptional* was usually the word he used, and that would burn me up because I'd been all over the world, and every country was amazing and beautiful and full of great people. Most of the time, church was just a place where I got worked up, and I expected that's why I felt none of the reverence was there.

Now, though, as we got close to Olodumare—a person knows a powerful god when she seems them—I felt more and more awed. One human form stood there, but I knew that this being was more than male or female, so I was very glad that Jed had taught me that some of his friends who didn't like to be labeled as one gender used the pronoun "they." Olodumare was beautiful, strikingly beautiful, but they were also gentle even as I knew that if they wanted to, they could take my breath right out of my body. They felt tender, like a tiny plant but also mighty like one of the giant chestnuts surrounding us. They were paradoxical and perfect, and I just wanted to sit at their feet and listen.

But as we got closer, I could see that Jed was talking and Olodumare nodding. They were listening to Jed with all of themselves, and I remembered the way Alonso had seen me when I was first seeable . . . the gift of that. I felt tears prick my eyes and quickly wiped them away before they hit my cheeks.

Just then, Olodumare looked at me and smiled, and I felt like everything from the bottoms of my feet to the back of my ribcage lit up. I couldn't help smiling back, and by the time I reached them on the steps, my cheeks hurt deliciously from grinning.

Olodumare stood, and I immediately felt like I should kneel. But they put a hand out and placed their palm on my forehead. I stood still and felt peace wash down my head to my shoulders. "Mavis," they said, and it felt like the first time anyone in the world had ever said my name. I didn't even feel silly when the tears streamed down my face.

I don't know what possessed me to do it, but I stepped forward and buried my face in Olodumare's chest, wrapping my arms around their waist. Without hesitation, I felt their arms reach around me and pull me close. I let myself sink into the best hug of my life.

When I stepped back, Olodumare was smiling. Then, I felt Oyá tug, and their gaze turned to my arm, where Oyá and they shared a look that carried more than I would ever understand.

"Time to begin." Olodumare's words rang through the town, and I felt The Shadow shift its attention this way. LaKeemba, Sharon, Adesina, Shelby, Alonso, The Wilsons, and Charlie all came out of the store, bottles of root beer in hand. Charlie handed one to Olodumare, who smiled and chugged the entire bottle in one gulp. I liked them more and more.

I looked at my friends as they all gazed back at me. I felt my left arm blaze then, not with pain but with the kind of heat that comes from drinking hot cocoa on a cold day. *Here we go*, I thought. Then, *I hope I don't have to run again.*

I looked down at my arm and saw the map standing out more brightly than it had ever before. I could see and feel, now, the outlines of every continent, sense the darkness where we stood but also in other places. The Shadow had split itself, and I realized where the phrase "Divide and Conquer" came from.

I remembered the plan Oyá and I had made, the one I'd been carrying with me all day, and I knew it was time for me to take charge. For a split second, I felt awkward; all these powerful people and two gods were standing nearby. Who was I to give orders? But I knew, the way sometimes we just know things, that this was my work, that it mattered that I do it.

More, though, I knew with a certainty I'd never had before that I wasn't alone. That we could do this together.

I raised my arms above my head and turned Oyá's face toward the map. Then, I breathed out the wind she commanded and felt the map unfurl into the air like a flag. It hung there above me, covering the sky, and I heard LaKeemba gasp.

I turned to my right, and there, beside me was Oyá, in her own flesh now, a lithe woman with long braids flowing down her back. She put a hand on my shoulder. "You did well, Mavis. Well done."

I caught Jed's eye, and he was grinning. Olodumare stood to his right as Oyá stood to mine, and I knew we were paired purposefully now as he and I had been since the day he was born. Some things that seem to just happen at random are actually carefully designed. I could see that now.

"Alright, Mavis? What's up?" Shelby was straight to the point, and I appreciated her push because if I'd had my way, I might have sat in that moment longer, enjoyed the quiet of my friends in this quiet for a little while. But I could feel The Shadow moving—behind me here in Capers—but also on the map above us. We had to get going.

"Alright, here's the plan," I said with more confidence than I felt. Oyá took my hand, and I felt a rush of strength. "We have to split up." I caught Mrs. Wilson's eye, and I could see the fear in her face. "I know. That's what happens before people start to die in those scary movies, right?"

Mrs. Wilson nodded, and I could see Jed agreeing.

"It is scary. It will feel like we are weaker because we are not together. But Oyá assures me that we are bound to one another, even when we are apart." I looked at my friend. "We can't be divided. Not ever. Not unless we choose to be."

"Forward and backward," LaKeemba said. "No matter when and where we go. We are wafted and woven together like a tapestry." She took Mrs. Wilson's hand. "Until we choose to separate."

I straightened my shoulders and looked up at the map. "You all can see the spots where The Shadow is growing. These are places in the world where people are focusing on their differences instead of looking for ways to love on each other. As I understand it"—I looked at Olodumare, who gave me a small nod —"our job is to go to each place where that ugliness is just starting to root in. We need to try to love it out."

My friends looked nervous, but no one protested.

"I don't know how to tell you to love well there, but I know you. You will find the way. You do you, and it'll be okay. I know that. It will always be okay."

I felt a bit like that Braveheart guy giving that wild speech before the battle, so I did what he did. I stood a little taller, and I looked each of my friends in the eye, willing my hope into them. They kept my gaze, and I knew. We were ready.

"I can't tell you how I know where to send you. The map is just telling me. You trust me though, right?" Every single head nodded, and I had to swallow hard to keep from crying again. "Alright then. Sharon and Shelby, you work on Belinda here." Some people might have thought I gave these strong women the easy job, but I knew they were in for it. From the look on their faces, they did too, but they didn't hesitate. They headed right for The Shadow without even waiting to hear where everybody else was going.

"Jed and Olodumare," I bowed my head just a little as I spoke their name, "Germany, 1908."

Jed nodded but looked confused.

I tried to clarify. "Hitler was rejected from art school that year. That's what a lot of folks think set him on this path of ugliness."

Jed's eyes got wide. He was going to meet Hitler. I couldn't tell if he was excited or terrified. I was glad he had Olodumare with him.

"You like some kangaroos?" I looked at Mr. Wilson.

"I prefer koalas, but roos will do." He smiled widely. "Australia then?"

"Yep. 1788. That's when the British started shipping prisoners and dropping them off there." I could feel The Shadow in that ugliness, the way the British had assumed that the aboriginal people of that land didn't matter. It made me shiver; it was so hateful. I pointed at Jed's dad, and Alonso took a deep breath and gave me a single, hard nod of his head and took Mr. Wilson's hand.

"Mrs. Wilson and LaKeemba, you're going to the Congo . . . in 1880."

LaKeemba's face went bright with joy. "To stop the Belgians from colonization of the kingdom."

"Right." Mrs. Wilson looked a little confused, but I knew LaKeemba would catch her up.

"Adesina and Charlie, you are headed to the Philippines in 1521 to see if you can convince—"

"We're going to meet Magellan?" Charlie's eyes were huge. Since coming to live with the Wilsons, he'd become a huge fan of history, especially the explorers. At first, he'd had a hard time when Alonso and the other folks from HeavenLand had explained that all that exploration had come with some serious costs, that most of it had been done so that white people could gain more land and wealth and that most people of color had suffered as a result. He still loved to study exploration, but he also realized that "advancement" doesn't always look like that to the people being advanced upon.

"You ready for the tropics, Charlie?" Adesina said with a gentle smile. Charlie took her hand, looking a little smitten.

I wanted to stay right there in that little town, to help Shelby and Sharon to get Belinda right if they needed us. But then, I wanted us all to finish, win, defeat, whatever it took, and then go back home together, where we could relax and slide into the lives we had been living.

I knew, though, that there was no going back. I couldn't unlearn what I knew, couldn't unbecome what the map and Oyá had helped me to be. Pining for the old days wasn't going to make the new ones any better.

I took a deep breath and started toward the ladder, which I could see just at the edge of town. We had some traveling to do.

10

W e had just over six hours left on the ship's clock, and we were all loaded up and headed out. I kind of wanted to ask LaKeemba what would happen if we were on the ship when its time ran out, but I figured I didn't want to know.

Marcus steered us all around the world and back and forth through time and within an hour, everyone was dropped off in their spot with a big hug from me and a firm handshake from Oyá. The plan was to come back and get them all before the ship —um—stopped being a ship. But if we couldn't get back in time, they each had a way back, a tree to walk around for most of them, or if you were Charlie, you got to come with Adesina, something I didn't think he'd mind one bit.

After everyone had left, I collapsed onto a bench, looking out over the Australian outback where we'd dropped Alonso and Mr. Wilson, who was trying out a *terrible* Australian accent as they descended the ladder.

We hovered there for a while. The map was telling me that things were happening. I could see the pockets of The Shadow swelling and shrinking around the world. We hadn't gone to every place The Shadow was growing, but for whatever reason, the map had picked where and when on its own. I just gave the marching orders.

I didn't like my role here. I was just supposed to sit on this ship and wait. The map had made that clear to me. I kept thinking about this wedding I had gone to when Jed was little. As I settled into a chair at the edge of the tent, I had seen a woman running around with a clipboard. She was telling everyone what needed to be done and when, and she looked really tired and frantic the whole time.

Then, when the ceremony had started, she hid behind a hedge at the back of the field where the ceremony took place. She had made this whole thing happen, but then, she couldn't be a part of it. Being the coordinator sucked.

I felt powerless and useless, even a little lazy. I was worried, especially about Jed—the boy was meeting Hitler—and I couldn't do a thing. And I couldn't sit still either. I kept standing up and looking over the edge of the ship and then sitting down again to pick at my fingernails.

Oyá rested quietly, her eyes closed, for a long time. But my restlessness must have eventually gotten to her because she stood and came over to where I was leaning over the stern of the boat, trying to see what was happening below us. "Do you see that highway, Mavis?"

In a break in the clouds, I could see the gray line of a roadway below us.

"It leads to a city called Darwin, over by the ocean, and it has led the way there for centuries, long before it was a road. It is what the aboriginal people here called a 'songline.'"

I craned my neck, trying to imagine the road without pavement, as a trail for feet rather than a road for vehicles.

Oyá gently took my arm and led me back to the bench. "For thousands of years, the indigenous peoples of Australia have found their way in the stars and in stories. They mapped these paths millennia ago, and then they'd tell the stories of the way to each other. These paths, these songlines, were the ways they traded with one another, saw other tribes, communicated over hundreds and hundreds of miles. Still, people use those ways because they are the best paths to reach a place in many parts of Australia."

I STOOD up and looked over the edge of the ship again. I said over my shoulder, "We always think that we are better than the people who came before us, don't we? That we have the best way."

Oyá stood and put her shoulder against mine. "Sometimes you do, Mavis. There are things that you have learned about over time that really matter—medicines, stories, the moon."

I took a deep breath.

"But yes, you often presume that now is better than then just because it's now."

I stood up and looked over the horizon. "Kind of like how white people often think the way we do things is better." I felt heavy then, not guilty exactly, just heavy. "That's where the map sent us, isn't it? To places where white people thought we knew better?"

"Or to places where white people thought they could take something because they were better."

"But how does Capers fit? Those are white people."

Oyá looked thoughtful. "They are. But they're poor, and whiteness often takes from poverty, too."

"Ugh." I wanted to be defensive, but I was finally beginning to get it. I was white. That didn't make me evil. It just gave me access to more things than other people. But it also gave me the chance to help make change, too. White supremacy was ugly. But being white just was a fact, just like being black was or being Asian was or being Native American was.

IT WAS a long quiet few hours. There wasn't much to chat about while your friends were out there trying to hold back evil and you're charged with keeping them safe. I checked the map almost constantly. It hovered over my head like one of those cartoon thought bubbles. Every once in a while, I'd look up to see what she had to say—check in with my eyes on what the rest of me was telling me. We were winning—if pushing back the edges of something is what we'd call winning. I kept hoping I'd see one pocket of The Shadow blink out and my friends' golden dots grow brighter, but that didn't happen. Instead, I just saw each gray spot grow a bit smaller or move a bit away. Never dislodged. Never dispelled. Just lessened.

At one point, we got the ship ready to go down to Germany. It looked like Jed and Olodumare might be losing ground a bit. Marcus had the ship turned and on its way when I saw a burst of light, and The Shadow shrank and backed off considerably from the hillside where it had been anchored. I let out a sigh.

When we were moving into the sixth and final hour of the ship, I could feel my friends waning, their energy flagging. They had made headway everywhere and everywhen they were, and now it was time to go get them, to pull them out, to let them rest.

As Marcus dropped the ladder over the side, I felt a great sadness. Oyá stirred from her seat at the prow and came to stand beside me where I looked down, waiting for Mr. Wilson and Alonso. "You have done good work, Mavis. Take heart."

I knew she was right. I knew I had done what I had been asked to do, that my friends had succeeded in the way that success goes in great battles—a little bit at a time. But I had hoped for some great win, a celebration that would rev us up and let us dance around like in the movies.

But then I thought of *Avengers: End Game,* the last movie that the Wilsons and I had seen together. There was a great victory there, a way of putting things right, but it was also sad. People did not come back. Everything did not get okay. Life just got set upright a bit again. It was good. It was not perfect. I felt like crying.

Oyá slid her arm around my waist and pulled me close. I pressed my head to hers, and I let the tears come and mingle with hers as I watched Mr. Wilson climb the ladder with Alonso after him.

MARCUS ZIPPED us around the world and history, and as each pair of friends climbed that ladder, Oyá and I greeted them with hugs and fresh glasses of ice-cold water. Everyone was silent, somber. Mrs. Wilson, in particular, looked drained. Her face was pale, and her hands were shaking a little. Oyá led her to Mr. Wilson and sat with them a while.

We had picked up Jed and Olodumare last, and once I saw the top of Jed's head on that ladder, I had found myself hoping they'd been able to work a miracle, that they were going to tell me that a good conversation with Hitler had wiped away his bitterness, had healed the pain that caused him to hate so bad. But as soon as I saw Jed's face, I knew the boy needed a hug, needed to be held up. I grabbed him and pulled him close, and he sobbed into my shoulder. "He couldn't hear us, Mavis. He couldn't hear us." I squeezed tighter and looked over his shoulder at Olodumare. The god was sorrowful, their face etched deep with lines of sadness. Sadness on the face of a god is a heavy thing.

In our last few minutes on the ship, Marcus flew us to Capers, and we quickly descended the ladder into the trees for the last time. Marcus's feet had just hit the ground when a wash of water, like a sudden rainstorm, poured over us and chilled us all through our clothes. The ship was gone.

As we walked into town, I could see Shelby and Sharon coming over the rise to meet us. They didn't look as battered as some of our friends did, but they were moving slowly, and their arms hung limp at their sides. "How'd it go?" I asked as we walked toward each other. It felt like a dumb question, like a question that didn't have enough space for a good answer.

But Shelby gave me a little smile. "It went." She looped her arm through mine, and we followed everyone into the general store, where Slot was waiting with the pot of coffee at the ready. "Slot here, he stood behind us the whole time, held us up kind of," Sharon said.

"Least I could do, my lady." I saw Sharon blush just a little as Slot winked at her.

Then, she headed straight back to the kitchen, and I could hear her moving pots and pans around. We had a good meal coming, and I started to go offer to help. But I thought maybe Sharon just needed some time alone. Jed grabbed the seat in the the front window, and his parents nestled in with him. Oyá and Olodumare perched on the counter together, and Adesina, Alonso, and LaKeemba were gathered around the table at the back, already well into a hand of gin rummy.

I headed over to where Charlie sat on the floor by the bags of flour. I didn't much fancy getting down there by him, but I thought it wise that neither of us be left too alone with our thoughts. I grunted my way down and propped myself against a post.

Then, I pulled out the "how'd it go" question again, and Charlie huffed. "Okay, I guess." He smiled a little. "It was good to meet Magellan, sort of. But then, we had to try and talk him out of what makes him Magellan." He looked up at me with tears in his eyes.

I put my arm around his shoulders. "I know, Charlie." I remembered the story I'd read about the folks who went to Thomas Jefferson's house and got all huffy because the tour guide talked about slavery. It's hard to see our heroes drop off their pedestals a little.

Charlie and I sat in silence a long time, the store quiet except for the occasional clang from the kitchen and the gentle swish of cards being dealt.

JEDIDIAH

I want to be able to tell all about Hitler, about how we changed the course of history like they say on all those TV shows. But I can't really. I mean, he was a sad, angry guy with brown hair. The moustache wasn't there yet.

He was polite enough. He listened, even offered us tea. But I could tell he wasn't really hearing us. I think you know what I mean. You know the way someone is listening—nodding and making sounds where they're supposed to but not really there for the words. That was Hitler. I think we came too late.

I thought about asking Mavis if we could go back, back to the first time the art school didn't let him in since he kept talking about that, but I didn't know if it would matter then either. It felt like we'd have to resteer him a hundred times all the way back to when he was a tiny kid to keep him from the way he was. We couldn't do that.

Mom and Dad sat with me there in that window a long time, and I kept thinking about all the ways they had helped me do the right thing. The time they'd made me rewrite a letter to our neighbor who was going away for the summer because I'd suggested he might lose some weight while he was gone. Mom had been so angry with me, and by this point, I knew why. But then, I just thought—I'm not even sure how I'd been taught that—that people weren't supposed to be fat, and it felt like humor and kindness to suggest that to him. I'm so embarrassed even now.

There was also the time my dad had stopped the car when he saw a van broken down on the side of the road one winter. He'd walked up to the passenger's side window, with me trailing behind him, and there was a sign that said, "Please call help." Two teenage girls were inside, scared and shaking. I wanted Dad to tell them to open the door so they could get in our car and get warm, but he walked back to our car and called the police. While we waited for them, he told me, "Sometimes, Jed, the best help you can give people is to let them be safe the way they know how." I didn't quite get it, though, until Mom explained, that night, that women had been hurt when their cars broke down and men pretended to help them. "Those girls were double-scared, Jed. Scared to be alone and cold on the side of the road, and scared of who might try to help them. Your dad did the right thing."

I suspected Hitler had never had anyone to teach him to really see people, to try to understand them, and that made me so sad. So very sad.

Olodumare and I had tried. We talked to him, and Olodumare even pushed a world of healing light around him. . . . It seemed like The Shadow got a little weaker then, but right around him, it just pulled in tighter, like it was a cape keeping him safe.

It had felt pretty hopeless, and a tiny part of me wanted to kill him right there just to keep him from killing so many other people. But I knew then that I'd just be grabbing The Shadow and pulling it close to me. That didn't seem like it would make things better, even though I had to wonder if we could have saved all those people if I had just been willing.

Thank goodness for Sharon's biscuits and chocolate syrup. When I smelled those biscuits cooking, I felt a little better, and it seemed like everyone else did, too.

11

I ate four biscuits totally smothered in chocolate syrup, and they helped the way home-cooked food always helps. Maybe I'd had low blood sugar. Or maybe Sharon had cooked a little something special into that chocolate. Either way, I was stronger, and it was time. Again. We had one more thing to do.

It felt like maybe we should huddle up like they do in all those sports movies that make you cry and wish you could hurl a ball-thing hundreds of yards. But I was anything but sporty, and it felt like I might never stop crying if I started now. So instead, I gave everyone a good look in the eye, and we all headed out, even Slot, who didn't seem to want to get far from Sharon's side.

That cloud of gray was still lingering over the end of town. Shelby said Belinda hadn't really been able to hear them when they'd tried to tell her that she was in danger and putting the town in danger, too. "She was just glassy-eyed and kept turning away when we tried to talk to her. It was like she didn't want to know she could do better." I knew the feeling well. Sometimes, it just was easier to keep going with what I knew than it was to try something else.

Charlie was walking along beside me, and I expected he knew, too. He had done an amazing thing to save this town, and I was proud of him, loved him. But it still felt like he was carrying a little backpack of guilt around. I slid my arm into his. Now wasn't the time to try to take that guilt away, but it's always the time to show a little kindness. I'd learned that.

As we approached The Shadow, I felt Oyá lean over to me. "Are you ready?"

I nodded, took a deep breath, and stretched out my right arm. She placed her warm hand on it and then squeezed gently. I felt her rather than saw her slide back into me. I suddenly felt braver, weightier, but lighter, too.

I turned over my shoulder to look at Jed and saw Olodumare whisper to him. Jed turned quickly then nodded. The next minute, the god was gone.

Jed caught my eye and raised his arm. There, in his suntanned skin, a face glowed. I winked at him.

We walked in a single line spread across the entire road the final few steps toward Belinda, her small gathering of townspeople, maybe twenty in all, and The Shadow. For a split second, my mind flashed to those Westerns that Mr. Wilson liked to watch so much, and I felt like we were about to have a showdown at high noon.

Belinda finally turned to look at us, and the people with her stepped behind her, leaving her as the very angry point of a people triangle. The Shadow seemed to turn and face us, too, although I could see nothing in that gray that felt human.

"We appreciate all you've done, but we'd thank you kindly to leave now." Belinda's voice was gravelly, and I was struck by how that Southern teaching about manners held strong even as a battle was about to ensue.

"We won't be going, Belinda. You still need us," I said and took a step forward. I felt my friends move with me. "The town is saved. Charlie and Esther did that. You don't have to fight so hard anymore."

"It'll never be safe. Somebody's going to always want us gone. Or invisible. I don't want to be invisible."

Oh man, did I know how she felt! "I see you, Belinda. We all do. We see Capers and the town full of nice folks that you've created here. You will always be here, even when you die. That's how life works." I could feel Oyá's vision soaring up into mine, and I saw the way Capers would and could be. The way the town would always stay on maps, always be passed down in stories, always be part of the people who knew it, even after the buildings were gone. "Places don't just disappear, Belinda. Not ever."

For just a second The Shadow shifted back, but then, what felt like a hot rush of despair blew over me, and I staggered. I looked up at my friends and felt hope again.

"No. No, we won't. Ain't nobody cared about us before, and nobody will care about us then unless we make them." Belinda's voice was very loud, and it echoed around the hills.

For a second, I thought of Idanre, wondered if we should retreat to a hollow and make our stand. But then Oyá spoke, "Not here, Mavis. We don't need a refuge yet. Here, we are on the attack." I gave one brisk nod and looked hard at Belinda.

"We care about you and about Capers, Belinda. We care a lot," Jed said. "I love this town. I've always wanted to go into a general store just like yours and put my hands in bins of screws, get a soda, pick up some of that penny candy the older people at church talk about. Now I've done that, and I still love it."

For just a split second, it felt again like maybe The Shadow was lightening, like Belinda might be hearing.

Sharon said, "Child, I know what it feels like to think you only get to be what other people say you is. Believe me, I know it. But you ain't only that. You is you, whoever you choose to be, even if you can't be that all the time everywhere. Right in the middle of you, that's always you."

A slight bit more light was coming in around Belinda and her friends.

We were gaining. I thought maybe we could get The Shadow to let loose. I was gearing up to step over and hug Belinda when a shiny black car came down the road, and The Shadow grew very dark again. It felt like it smiled . . . at me.

Two men in dark-gray suits stepped out of the car, and I immediately thought of *Men in Black* and wished for Will Smith to arrive. But something told me these guys weren't here to help us.

"Belinda Specker? Thank you for calling us. The President is grateful for your cooperation."

I looked at Belinda and saw a slight smile cross her lips. It wasn't the kind of smile that made you smile back. I took a step backward.

"Of course, gentlemen. Let's go into my store up the road and talk."

I looked at LaKeemba and then Jed and then down at Oyá. None of us knew what was happening, but all of us knew this wasn't good.

We watched Belinda and her friends lead the two men past us and up to the store, The Shadow wrapped around all of them now.

As soon as they were out of earshot, Charlie whispered, "They can't see The Shadow!"

"I guess not," I said. "What do we do now?"

A silence settled among us. Jed walked over and sat down on the steps of the barbershop, and soon, all of us were gathered on that tiny porch, sitting with our knees bent and our backs against the shop wall and the porch posts. I hoped Lou the barber didn't mind.

Finally, Charlie sighed and said, "Maybe I should undo the time pocket."

My first instinct was to say, "No," but then I wondered. Maybe it was just better to let the town go, to take away the place where Belinda felt like she had some power. Maybe then she'd let go of whatever ugliness she was going to do. But as I sat with that idea, I knew it wasn't right either. It would never be right to let other people suffer just because one person did, not if we could help it.

I leaned my head back against the barbershop wall and sighed. It felt like we were all just going to sit there and see what Belinda did. Like we didn't have much of a choice.

But then, in the distance, I heard bells and hoofbeats. I sat up and saw Charlie and Jed lean forward and exchange a glance.

Then, up over the hill came Hercules's wagon. It looked just the same as it had back in our time. The promise was still there —"Hercules Pettit—Peddler of All the Things You Never Knew You Needed." Man alive, did we need something we hadn't known we needed. Hercules looked calm there on the front of that wagon, and he was smiling to beat the band. I felt better just seeing him.

He jumped off the front of the wagon, spry as a teenager, and walked around the back before coming over to us with a small box in his hand. He walked right up to Charlie and handed it to him. "Thought you might be needing this, Charlie."

"Um, thank you?" Charlie studied the box carefully, looking at all the sides of it without turning it over. "Sorry if this is rude, but what is it?"

Hercules sat down beside Charlie on the step and said, "Well, open it, kid."

Charlie glanced over his shoulder at Mr. Wilson, who gave him a nod. "Go ahead, Charlie. Hercules's first gift was good, right?"

Slowly, Charlie undid the brass clasp on the front of the box and lifted the lid. I couldn't quite see into the box from where I sat, so I leaned forward just as Charlie lifted out a bright red ribbon with a gold medallion dangling from the end. He looked just about as puzzled as I felt. What was that thing, and why did Charlie need it?

I was about to ask Hercules that very thing, but Charlie's face grew bright. He reached into his back pocket and took out Ruth's journal. I had all but forgotten about the book Charlie had found.

Charlie opened it and then held the ribbon and medallion over it like he was going to place it in the seam at the center of the pages.. The book began to flip its pages, and we watched as it turned each one slowly, like it was reading itself. Eventually, it stopped about three-quarters of the way through, and Charlie placed the ribbon in the valley of the pages. A gentle flare of light came from a line of handwriting halfway down on the right-hand page.

Charlie read, "When you find this line, Charlie, it will be time. It will be nice to finally meet you." His brow furrowed, and he looked at Hercules and then over at Alonso.

"Look, Charlie," Adesina said.

There, walking up the road, was a young woman about Mrs. Wilson's age with a walk like a bounce that was just like Charlie's. I couldn't believe it.

Charlie stood up and began to slowly walk toward the woman. Then, he broke into a run, and so did she. But instead of hugging when they met each other, they just stopped about two feet apart and stared.

We were all staring too. I leaned over to Jed and said, "Did you know Charlie had a sister?" It had to be his sister. . . .

"That's not his sister. That's his mom."

If I had been a cartoon character, my jaw would have literally dropped to the ground. I took a breath, though, and realized it made sense. We'd never met Charlie's mom, but here she was, which meant that she was probably magic too.

After she and Charlie stared for a while and then finally hugged, they walked back over to us. "Everyone, this is my mother. Mama, this is, um, everyone."

She smiled. "Nice to meet you, everyone. I'm Ruth. Unless you want to call me Mama too." She spoke with a slight Irish accent.

I liked her already.

"We've met before, haven't we Charlie?" Ruth said as she and Charlie took a seat at the edge of the barbershop porch.

Charlie looked puzzled. "Just that once when I was seven. You came by to see Judith in the kitchen about some pies, you said." He smiled. "But even then, I knew it was you. At least I think I did. You felt familiar somehow."

She reached up to put her arm around Charlie's shoulders. "I checked in a lot, but that was the one time you saw me. Maybe I had wanted you to see me." She turned to us then. "Charlie's dad has a thing about magic people, but then I expect you know that. I had to leave to protect Charlie and myself. But I've stayed close. Walking back to him whenever I got worried about what his daddy might have been doing to him. I need to thank you all for getting my Charlie out of there. I'd tried before, but Poke's men always stopped me. It took all of you to free him. Thank you."

LaKeemba said, "You don't need to thank us. We're glad to have Charlie."

Mrs. Wilson stepped forward. "We've been thrilled to have him with us." She looked at Mr. Wilson too. "And we'd be happy to have you come to the farm, too, if you'd like."

Ruth smiled. "That's mighty kind of you. But no, if Charlie is ready, he and I have other business when we're done here. Don't we, Charlie?"

I looked at the red-headed teenager. "Charlie? You've never mentioned any business." I wanted to be happy he'd found his mom, but I didn't like the thought of him leaving. Guess that's what gave my question a *tone,* as Mrs. Wilson would call it.

I felt a hand take mine and looked over to see Hercules beside me. "Charlie received a gift much like yours, Mavis."

Charlie held up his arm, and there, in his skin, I saw writing, handwriting. "I don't understand." I looked into Charlie's face, and he looked a little older, a little wiser than before.

"Mom's journal. Well, I didn't know it was Mom's then. It came into me like the map came into you."

Hercules squeezed my hand. "The things I distribute, Mavis, they become a part of the person who gets them. You got the map. Charlie got the journal—"

"But Charlie found that journal. You didn't give—"

"Nothing is ever just found, Mavis. The peddler's voice was soft but clear. "Nothing is ever lost either."

I wanted to think about that a little more, but I'd have to ponder later. We had work to do, The Shadow to stop.

Ruth spoke then. "Charlie has some of my gift. I can't stop time, but I can slow it or speed it up. That's why I'm here. Charlie did the work to set Capers out in a pocket. I'm here to help you keep it there."

"So Belinda is trying to fight that?" Shelby said.

"Yes, she wants to rip open the pocket. That would be bad enough, but I know—you probably do too—that when someone figures out they have that kind of power, and when that power comes with an ugliness along with it, that this won't be the last thing she'll hurt."

"She's trying to undo the work we all did," I said it almost as a whisper. "Even back at HeavenLand."

Ruth nodded.

I looked at my friends. "We can't let that happen."

Alonso smiled at me. "We won't."

Hercules was still holding my hand, and he squeezed it again. "You've got your gift. Charlie has his. Now it's time for Jed to get his own." He handed Jed a piece of what looked like pencil lead about the size of a piece of chalk.

Jed looked at the gift and grinned. "Got it. Let's go."

Everyone else started walking, and Hercules was pulling me along as I said, "Go? Go where? We need a plan."

"Sometimes, Mavis, the best plan is just to get doing." Hercules smiled.

JEDIDIAH

As we walked toward the store, that little piece of charcoal zipped into me and left me feeling like I'd had a whole case of Red Bull. Then, I knew I had to get to the edge of town right away.

As I sprinted past the store and down the mountain to the final building in town, I heard my friends coming behind me. They had no idea what was going on, of course, but I loved that they came along anyway. They had my back.

I could see it then, shimmering, the pocket that Charlie and Esther had built. It was there, just at the edge of the forest, where the clearing for the town gave way to trees. I rested my fingertips against it and began to draw. This time, I wasn't using my fingers. I was using my whole body—it kind of felt like this one time I'd danced at the Drive-By Truckers concert with Mom and Dad and found myself totally lost in the music. I didn't know what I was doing, but I felt my way along.

First, I drew small groups of men walking the ridgeline, their clothing made of animal skins. They were hunting, and then, they'd take their game home to their villages by the rivers below us. The image was like a giant mural hanging in the air. I was pulling colors from my memory and filling in the outline the charcoal in me was creating. "The Monacans," I heard Sharon say.

I moved on around the mountaintop and sketched first a few armed men coming over the mountains, and even I recognized these guys as Lewis and Clark. Then, my hands danced in the air and drew families coming up the mountains and cutting down trees to build cabins and planting gardens. Children played in the woods, and eventually, these people found each other and a few more folks joined them. Then, I found myself drawing the building of the general store in Capers. Finally, as I came back to where I'd started, I drew Capers as it was now.

When I was done, I wanted to just lay down on the ground and sleep, but I knew we weren't finished yet. I could feel The Shadow coming over the mountaintop towards us, and I needed to be ready. We all did.

12

J ed's drawing was amazing and not just because he had drawn it with his bare hands in the air. The kid had talent, well, talent and magic. The people in that drawing were moving like they were alive. Maybe they were alive. I wanted to look at what Jed had created for a long time, but of course, we didn't have a long time. In fact, we didn't have any time at all.

As we turned back toward town, Belinda and her cloud were coming toward us. And any pretense of good manners was gone from Belinda's face. That woman was angry, very angry. "Ya'll don't take a hint, do you? I told you we'd handle this, but you can't mind your own business. Now, we have to mind it for you."

She flicked her hand toward us like she was telling us to shoo, and a whip of the cloud came shooting out toward us, hard and fast. LaKeemba stepped forward and put out an arm, and the whip stopped in mid-air and trembled like it was pushing against something too heavy for it to move. LaKeemba looked calm, but I could see her jaw was clenched.

Sharon went forward then with the Wilsons on either side of her, and as she raised her arms over her head, they each placed a hand on her shoulder. From her open palms, a pulse of light moved farther and farther into the cloud, pushing it back from in front of LaKeemba's steady arm. Alonso stepped forward and placed one hand on Mr. Wilson's back and one on LaKeemba's, and The Shadow retreated farther.

I saw all this happen out of the corner of my eye because I was focused on Belinda, whose body looked like it might explode from anger. Her face was bright red, and she was shaking. She was looking right at me and coming closer.

I started to back up, out of instinct more than anything, but then I felt two hands take mine, and I saw Charlie and Jed beside me. Jed had his hand in Hercules's, and Hercules had his other hand around LaKeemba's bicep. Ruth was holding her son's hand, and Shelby took her other. Adesina was beside Shelby. I could feel Oyá rising in me, and when Olodumare's charge reached out to her, it felt like I'd been jolted by gentle lightning. We were ready.

Belinda's crew, including the two men in suits, who looked a little dazed, formed their own line to face off against us, and I thought of all those battles in the American Revolution where the British stood in a broad line with orders to shoot only when the enemy was close enough to see "the whites of their eyes." I got the camaraderie of it all, but this fighting position felt really dumb—like we were basically those games at a carnival, where you use a toy gun to take them down. I didn't want The Shadow to win a giant teddy bear though.

Fortunately, it seemed like we were holding the line. I felt Oyá shift in my arm, turning to look at me, and I dragged Charlie's arm up to look at her. "Now, Mavis," she said.. I glanced at Jed and then at Charlie, and the three of us stepped forward, bringing our friends with us.

"Ms. Belinda," Jed's voice was quavering, but it was loud. "Ms. Belinda, you don't have to do this. We've protected Capers, and I think we did it the way you wanted."

Belinda's eyes flickered to Jed just momentarily, but then they slid back and unfocused as if listening to something we couldn't hear.

I felt Charlie and Ruth shift near me, and they'd locked arms so their hands were free. Charlie was tending the pocket of time, keeping it whole even as the tendrils of The Shadow tried to pick it apart above LaKeemba's power. Next to him, Ruth extended her arms again and again as if pushing against a pile of tumbling ribbon of satin, and I could see Charlie shift forward a little each time she pushed. Ruth was holding him up as he worked. Adesina let her hand rise and fall with Ruth's arm.

Shelby spoke next, even as we took another step forward. "Belinda. Listen to me. I know what it's like to have people try and tell you how you have to live, what you have to do for them. Believe me, I know. But this ain't the way to fix that. This giving into the ugliness, it's only going to destroy you—it won't save your town. It won't save anybody."

When Belinda spoke, her voice echoed off the hills around us. "I'd rather it die than be taken."

I felt a shiver run up my spine. Those were not the words of a woman who could be talked out of something. Still, I had to try. "Belinda, for most of my life, almost no one saw me. It felt normal to me until it didn't. But then, my normal changed, and being seen was terrifying. I almost wanted to go back, to hide again. It took some time, and then I got used to it. Nothing is the same, it's true. But it's better. I have all these people." I meant what I said, felt stronger for just saying it. But it wasn't working, I could tell. If anything, Belinda's face was redder, angrier. "Belinda, it doesn't have to be like this."

Her face was rigid with rage, but beneath that, I thought I could see how sad she was, how brokenhearted. I got it. I really did. It's a lot easier to be angry than it is to be so very sad.

From the corner of my eye, I saw a swath of gray coming around. "They're trying to flank us," Adesina shouted as she spun and tossed out a web of light toward The Shadow. She, Ruth, Charlie, Jed, and I rotated just a bit to face the arm-thing of The Shadow, but I didn't take my eyes off Belinda.

Adesina pushed The Shadow back and around, so we were all in a line again, and I caught a glimpse of Mrs. Wilson and Sharon shifting to keep the left side of The Shadow's energy from coming around behind us on that end, too.

Charlie and Ruth were still weaving. LaKeemba, Alonso, Mr. and Mrs. Wilson, and Sharon were still holding back the bulk of The Shadow's force. We were steady, but we couldn't keep this up forever. For now, though, we were holding ground, maybe even gaining a little.

The standoff continued for what seemed like hours. The Shadow would try an attack, and we'd counter. We'd push it back a bit, and then it would surge, powered—at least it looked to me—by Belinda's anger. With each minute, her face grew redder and more hateful. I thought she might break her teeth; she was clenching her jaw so hard.

Eventually, though, I knew we were fading, and we were stuck. No one was giving ground, and it felt like Belinda and The Shadow might best us. Sadly, I wondered if anger might have more stamina than love.

But then, I felt a warmth spread from my left hand up into my body and down my right arm. When I looked over, I saw Hercules, his arms locked with LaKeemba and Jed, speaking.

"In the end, love wins. It always has. It always will. In the end, love wins. It always has. It always will."

Over and over, he repeated this phrase in the kind of musical tone I'd heard monks use on those mesmerizing videos of them praying. With each repetition, I felt lifted, buoyed up by something I couldn't describe but maybe would call hope.

We took a step forward, and then, as if all they needed was for us to show our own determination, Oyá and Olodumare surged forth, taking their own forms on the ground in front of us. They stood with their legs wide apart, and their arms spread above them. "You may not come this way," Olodumare's voice boomed around the mountains.

Belinda took a stumbling step back, and I saw her eyes grow wide as Olodumare and Oyá took another step forward, us right behind them.

"You may not come this way." Oyá's voice pushed The Shadow and its people again.

"You are not welcome here." I was as surprised as anyone that my voice was rich and deep, not god-like by any means, but powerful. I led our line forward another step.

One by one, we spoke words of unwelcome, and step by step, The Shadow, Belinda, and their gathered crew stepped back. I could feel the power surging through us, knew that if we wanted, we could obliterate The Shadow and take Belinda and her followers along with it. Part of me wanted to just blow them all away, send them all into dust. But a larger part of me, the part of me that believed what Hercules was saying, resisted that urge. Killing was not the answer. Love was.

Mrs. Wilson was the last one to speak. "You have no place here. There is no discord here any longer. Be gone." She raised her left hand and passed it over her head in an arc, and just like that, The Shadow dissipated completely.

Belinda collapsed to the ground, her body wracked with tears. Her people sat on the grass beside her and wept, broken, battered folks.

I rushed over to Belinda and bent down to help her up. She smacked my arm away. "Leave me alone. I don't want your help. I don't *need* your help."

I felt tears prick my eyes, and then a hand settled in the middle of my back. "You don't want it, Belinda. But it is always here for if you do." LaKeemba steered me away and back toward town.

THE WALK back to the store only took a few minutes, but it felt like days. We'd won, in some sense, but if this was victory, I wasn't sure I wanted much of it.

Everyone sat around at the counter and the table in the general store, silent and slouching. We were tired, and if I hadn't seen The Shadow disappear myself, I'd say we were the ones who were defeated. After a few minutes, I finally got up, grabbed sodas from the cooler, and handed them around. I figured I could visit the store again soon—presuming that someone kept it up, that is—and settle up then.

"This sucks," Jed said, and I looked to Mrs. Wilson for her usual reprimand about using better words for things. But she just nodded because of course, Jed was right. This did suck.

But then, I looked over to Hercules, this tiny man with a ring of white hair around his smooth bald skin. He was smiling. Not a smile of victory or even of happiness. No, his smile was one of resolve, of contentment. It reminded me of one of Mrs. Wilson's favorite sayings, "All shall be well, and all manner of things shall be well."

I walked over and sat next to Hercules, and he took my hand in his again and held it in his lap. "Thank you, Mavis."

I looked at him and squinted. "Why are you thanking me? You brought us the gifts we needed."

He smiled at me gently. "Ah, but lots of gifts go unused. I give people a lot of things, things they need, things that will help them be more of who they were made to be, things that will even give them joy, and sometimes things that also come with a fair amount of heartache, too. But they're all good gifts, even the hard ones."

He was looking out across the store now like he were seeing every one of those gifts he'd distributed, and even though he was smiling, I could see a little sadness in his eyes too.

Then he gave his head a little shake and turned to look at me. "But you, Mavis, you used your gift, and you used it well." He gave my a hand a squeeze with both of his.

"I don't know about that. I didn't know what I was doing." I still wasn't great at taking a compliment.

He gave a great chortle. "None of us do, Mavis. Do you think I had any idea what to do when that wagon showed up at my door all those years ago? I was just sitting there, eating an apple. It was September, and it was my first apple of the year. I still remember even though that was sixty-seven years ago. This old, old man—kind of like me, I guess," he said with a little laugh, "rode up on this wagon, got off, and said, 'Here you go, Hercules. It's an adventure.' And then he walked off down the mountain."

I tried to imagine a teenage version of Hercules sitting there with a half-eaten apple in his hand and a wagon waiting for him. "What did you do?"

"Well, I did what seemed the right thing. I finished my apple, and then I got up in that wagon and got going. Nothing else was holding me back, so I just went. Been going ever since. Expect I'll keep going until I find my own apple eater to hand the wagon to on down the road a piece."

I looked over at him and smiled. "I hope that's a long piece of road between now and then."

"We never know then, do we, Mavis? We never know."

"You got that right."

Eventually, we all headed to our beds, not sure what tomorrow would need but certain we needed sleep.

13

The next morning, I woke up feeling rested but restless. It was my least favorite kind of wake-up. I almost wished I'd had a bad night's sleep to match the aching worry that hit my chest as soon as thought entered my brain.

Sharon was already up and moving, a toothbrush extending from her cheek as she said, "Pffkaff?"

I smiled and waited for her to finish. "You were saying?"

"Pancakes. Do you want pancakes? I'm headed over to make a mess for everybody."

I didn't feel much like eating, which was rare, but I figured I'd probably need the sustenance. "Sure. I'll help."

We made our way over to the store as the sun began to come up over the tops of the mountains around us. LaKeemba and Shelby were already there with coffee mugs on the front porch. "Inside," Shelby gestured over her shoulder, and I could smell the blessed scent of rich caffeine coming from the kitchen.

Sharon made quick work of prepping the batter while I fixed us two creamy, sweet mugs from the coffee percolator on the stove.

Then, we took turns flipping pancakes on the griddle. It was a hot job, and I kept wondering how people had managed to cook full meals over wood heat until the invention of the modern oven with its easy "off" switch.

By the time we were done, everyone else had wandered in, looking about how I felt: exhausted and sad. Charlie's hair stood up like he had been in a wind tunnel, and the circles under Jed's eyes were a deep purple. I wondered if he'd slept at all.

As everyone ate, I expected LaKeemba to have some words, some wisdom to help us all. But she slid one piece of pancake in her mouth after the other, her head tilted to one side as if she were thinking.

I was watching her eat when Hercules began to talk. "I've been at this a long time, longer than all of you, I think. I've seen a lot riding through the years this way. You all did well yesterday. You sent that Shadow on its way, for now, and sometimes that's the best you get. I've never seen one of those storybook endings in real life. I kind of think 'happily ever after' is a lie or at least not the whole truth. Nothing's quite that simple. But you did well." He looked at me and smiled.

We ate quietly for a few more minutes, and then Mrs. Wilson spoke up, "I'm so proud of all of you. You were braver than I ever imagined I could be, and that made me brave. Thank you."

Her words brought out a few more smiles, and as we cleaned up the tables and put the store to rights, the mood felt a little brighter.

IT ALSO FELT LIKE GOODBYE. It was time to go home. I knew it, and I think everyone else knew it too.

I needed to do one more thing, and apparently, Jed had the same idea I did because we both ducked around the side of the store at the same time.

"I hate saying goodbye," he said, and I thought he might cry. I kind of wished he would. Tears are good things, I was learning.

"Me, too, but we can't keep them for ourselves."

"No, you can't." Olodumare's voice tingled my ribs as they appeared in front of us. "We wouldn't let you if you tried, but we are glad you aren't trying."

I gave a small smile to him and then at Oyá by his side. I'd felt her draw herself out of me a few moments before. "Thank you." It felt like not enough to give back to her but also the only thing that mattered.

"You are most welcome, Mavis. Most welcome. We will always be here with you. You just need to ask for us." I nodded, and then I hugged her tight. She put her hands on my back and squeezed.

Olodumare gave Oyá a slim nod, and then, they turned and walked into nothing. I dropped my arm over Jed's shoulder as we stared after their absence before we turned back to our friends who waited on Main Street.

Charlie was standing near Adesina, and I watched him hug her before she waved and stepped off into the sky. Ruth had her hands on her son's shoulders before he turned and buried his face in her shoulder. His head jerked up quickly though, but it took a minute for me to hear it—bells. He must have slipped out.

There he came over the mountain in his wagon. As he rode up, he tossed Charlie a bright red apple and gave me a wink before stepping down and handing one to Ruth too. "You ready?"

Charlie only looked confused for a flash of a second before he nodded. Then, he looked at his mom with hope shining in his eyes.

"Of course, we're ready," she said with a smile. "We've been waiting our whole lives for this, haven't we Charlie?"

Then, they climbed up on the wagon seat, where Charlie took the reins. "We'll be seeing you," he said with a catch in his throat. It felt like he wanted to say more, but I could see the water pooled in his eyes, and Charlie wasn't one to cry. He'd learned too early that tears could be dangerous.

"Yes, yes we will, Charlie." Mr. Wilson gave him a thumbs-up, and Mrs. Wilson smiled through her tears. "Be safe."

Then, they were off over the mountain and out of sight.

TOGETHER, the rest of us began the walk down the mountain. I almost stopped because I didn't know how we'd get home. The ship was gone, and Oyá had left.

But then, I looked down and saw that Oyá had left me her map. The golden glow of us lit up my skin. Under it, the blue of home shone. Mrs. Wilson looped her arm in mine and then wrapped her husband's hand in her own. Each of my friends took another's hand, and we formed a circle there at the edge of the woods. Then, I placed my thumb and index finger on my skin and took us home.

JEDIDIAH

The day after Mavis carried us all back to the farm, Dad and I drove back to the cabin to get our stuff. No one had noticed we were gone, of course, because that's one rule of time travel that is true—time doesn't flow the same everywhere. In our time, we'd only been gone a few hours.

Dad suggested I take one last dip in the lake. I suspected he wanted a bit of time to himself, and I loved the way swimming made me feel, like all the hard things were carried away. I jumped in, wearing my good shorts even though I knew Mom would be less than happy.

I swam out a ways and then let myself float on my back, my arms splayed out beside me. If it hadn't taken me a little bit of concentration to stay afloat—"You're too skinny to float good," Mavis always said—I probably would have dozed off.

I kind of thought I had when I saw Oyá's face above me. She wasn't there, not the way she had been before. She sort of seemed like she was coming through a mirror or something. "Jed." Her voice was kind but serious.

"Jed, I am glad you are resting. You will need it. Be ready. Watch for the signs. Avoid the shadows. Tell the others. We will need you." She smiled, and then she was gone.

I floated a while longer because it hadn't seemed urgent, her words, and because I needed time to make sense of them. But eventually, when my fingers started to get pruney, I made my way to shore. As soon as my feet hit the mud bottom, I felt it. It was awful.

I sprinted to the cabin. We had to get ready. All of us.

ALSO BY ANDI CUMBO-FLOYD

THE MAGIC PEOPLE - BOOK 1

The Boy Who Could See Secrets

ALSO BY ANDI CUMBO-FLOYD

THE STEELE SECRETS SERIES

Steele Secrets

Charlotte and the Twelve

Silence at the Lock

GHOSTS. SPELLS. PEOPLE WITH WILD ABILITIES.

If these are your faves, then come on over and get all the magical realism books your TBR can handle. Weekly emails of magical realism and fantasy, especially for young adults and the young at heart. Plus, a few notices about my own books, too.

Join my newsletter here:

andilit.com/magical-realism

ABOUT THE AUTHOR

Andi Cumbo-Floyd is a writer, editor, and historian who lives in the Blue Ridge Mountains with her husband, son, three dogs, and three cats. She writes regularly at andilit.com.

facebook.com/andilitwriter

twitter.com/andilit

CPSIA information can be obtained
at www.ICGtesting.com
Printed in the USA
LVHW052343071019
633408LV00001B/249/P